my LiTTLE PONY™

Friendship is Magic 2

My Little Pony: Friendship is Magic 2

Written by
Katie Cook

Art by
Andy Price

Colors by
Heather Breckel

Letters by
Robbie Robbins

Edited by
Bobby Curnow

Cover by
Stephanie Buscema

Digest Edits by
Justin Eisinger & Alonzo Simon

Digest Design by
Neil Uyetake

For Grayson, my own lil' Cutie Mark Crusader. -Katie

With great love to friends and family, for my wife Alice and our cats Spooky, Tabitha, Boris, Bela, and Mina. And above all, especially for Sam. -Andy

Special thanks to Erin Comella, Robert Fewkes, Joe Furfaro, Heather Hopkins, Pat Jarret, Ed Lane, Brian Lenard, Marissa Mansolillo, Donna Tobin, Michael Vogel, and Michael Kelly for their invaluable assistance.

IDW founded by Ted Adams, Alex Garner, Kris Oprisko, and Robbie Robbins

ISBN: 978-1-61377-860-9

17 16 15 14 1 2 3 4

IDW® Licensed By: Hasbro

Ted Adams, CEO & Publisher
Greg Goldstein, President & COO
Robbie Robbins, EVP/Sr. Graphic Artist
Chris Ryall, Chief Creative Officer/Editor-in-Chief
Matthew Ruzicka, CPA, Chief Financial Officer
Alan Payne, VP of Sales
Dirk Wood, VP of Marketing
Lorelei Bunjes, VP of Digital Services

Become our fan on Facebook **facebook.com/idwpublishing**
Follow us on Twitter **@idwpublishing**
Check us out on YouTube **youtube.com/idwpublishing**
www.IDWPUBLISHING.com

Originally published as MY LITTLE PONY: FRIENDSHIP IS MAGIC issues #3–4.

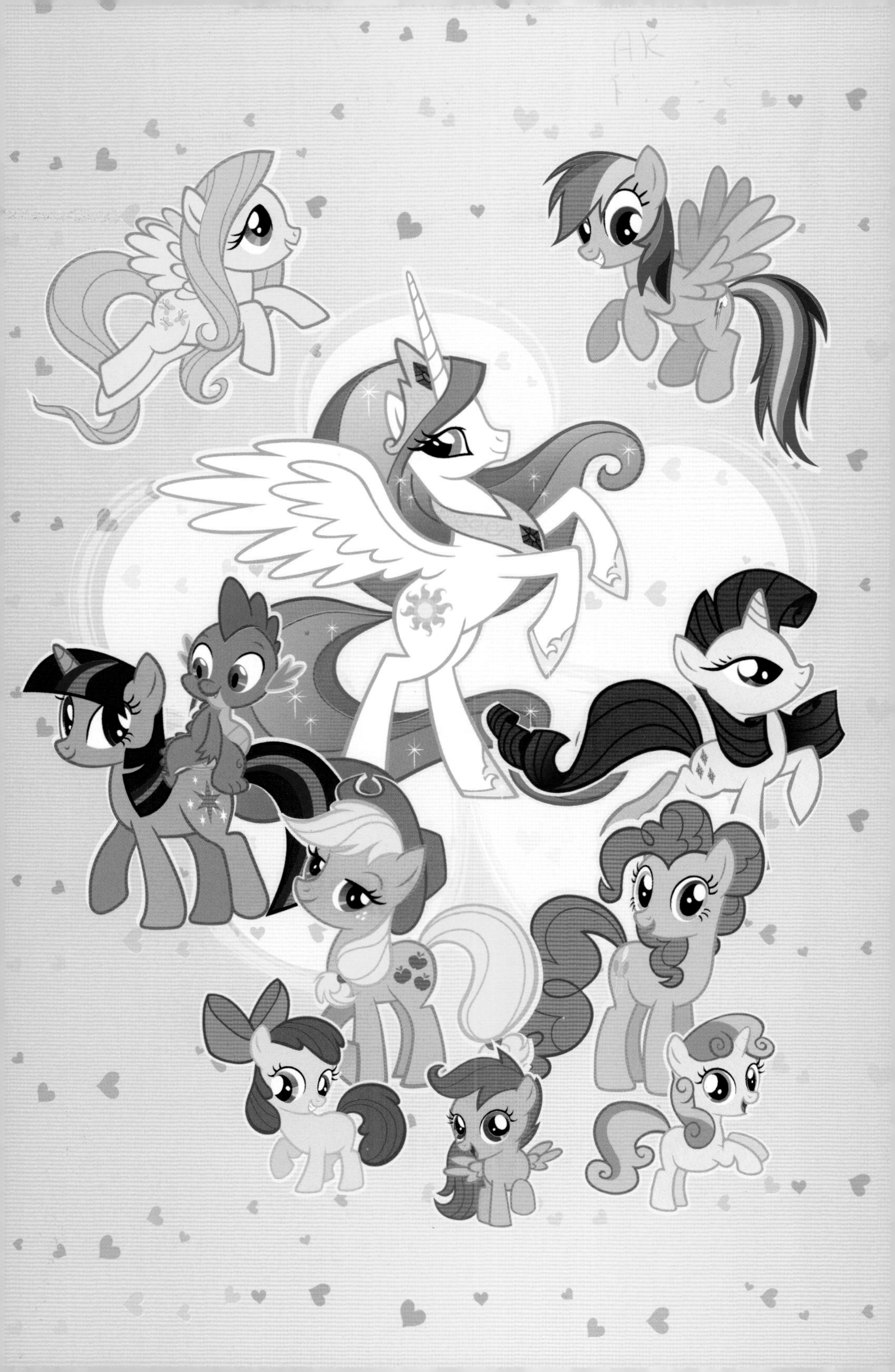

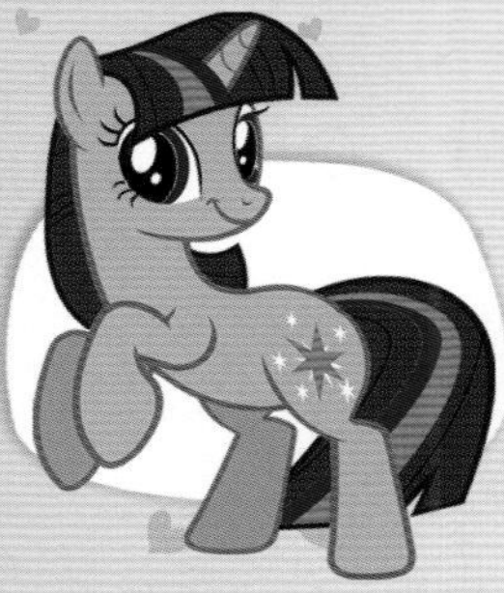

TWILIGHT SPARKLE

Twilight Sparkle is a unicorn with a big heart. Even though she prefers to have her muzzle stuck in a book, she's always willing to put her work aside to help her friends! She's also one of the most magically gifted unicorns there is thanks to her studies and the personal guidance of Princess Celestia.

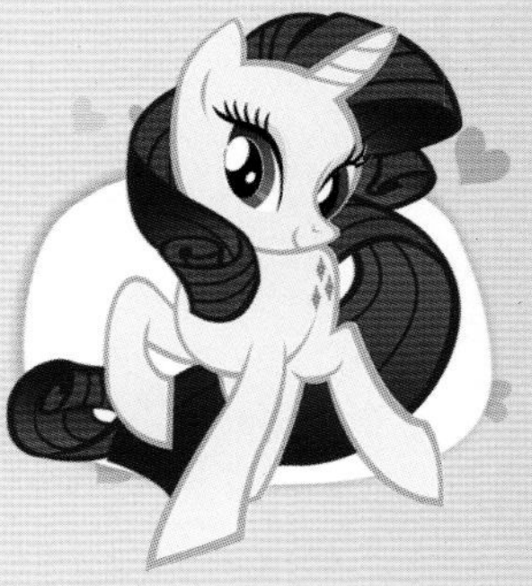

RARITY

Rarity is a unicorn who has dedicated her life to making beautiful things... She's a fashion designer in Ponyville and has aspirations to be "the biggest thing in Equestria." She has big dreams, but she's very dedicated to her Ponyville friends who have always been there for her.

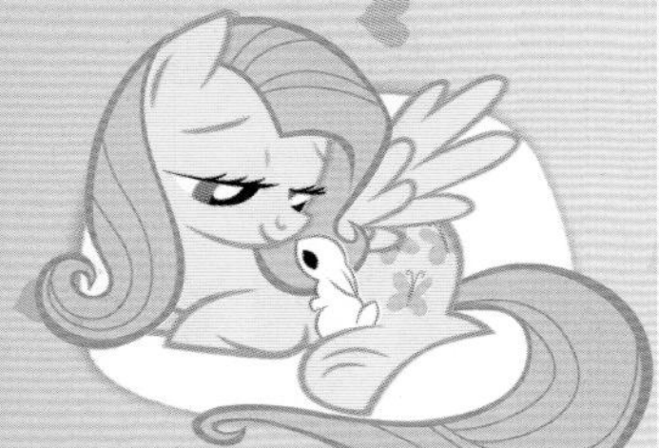

FLUTTERSHY

Fluttershy is a shy pegasus with a gentle hoof. Her love and understanding of animals is almost legendary to the ponies around her. She's calm and collected, even when faced with some of the scariest beings in the Everfree Forest!

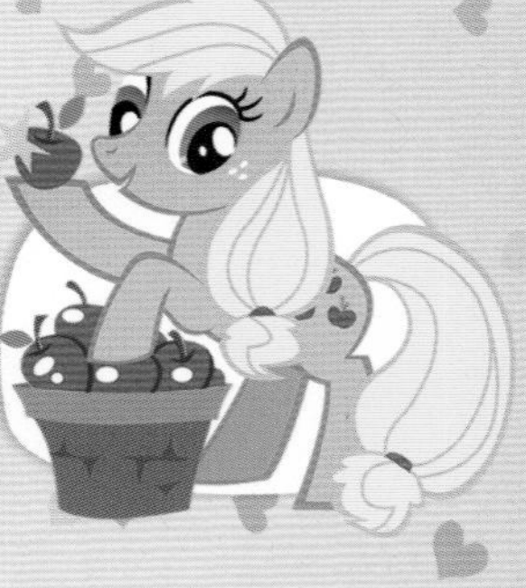

APPLEJACK

Applejack is a pony you can trust. She's the hardest worker in all of Ponyville and will always be there to lend a helping hoof! She and her family run Sweet Apple Acres, the foremost place to acquire apples and apple-related goodies in Ponyville.

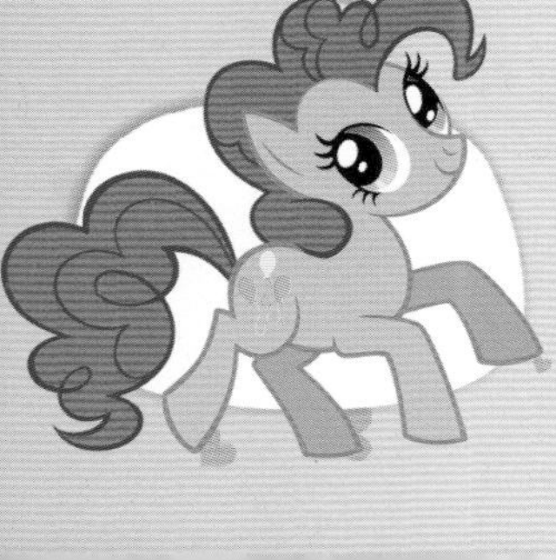

PINKIE PIE

Pinkie Pie is a pony that likes to PAR-TAY. Friendly, funny... and maybe a little weird, Pinkie Pie is always on hoof for a celebration for any occasion! She's always there with a smile and an elaborate cake, even if she's just saying "thanks for pet-sitting my alligator."

RAINBOW DASH

Rainbow Dash is the fastest pegasus around... and she KNOWS it! Never one to turn down a challenge, she's always ready to seize the day (in the spirit of friendly competition of course!).

SPIKE

Spike the Dragon is the pint-sized assistant to Twilight Sparkle. Besides helping her out in the Ponyville library, he helps her practice spells and with the duties of her daily life... he may be in the designated role of "helper," but he's also her dear friend.

QUEEN CHRYSALIS

Queen Chrysalis is the Queen of the Changelings. After a failed attempt to take over Equestria, she now has her sights set on Twilight and her friends.

PRINCESS CELESTIA

Princess Celestia is the ruler of Equestria and Twilight Sparkle's mentor. Princess Celestia is kind, gentle, and powerful... everything she needs to be to rule and protect her kingdom.

THE CUTIE MARK CRUSADERS

The Cutie Mark Crusaders are comprised of Sweetie Belle, Apple Bloom, and Scootaloo. These young fillies have yet to earn their cutie marks (the image on a pony's flank depicting their special talent!) and they are dashing through task after task together with the sole purpose of finding what makes them unique.

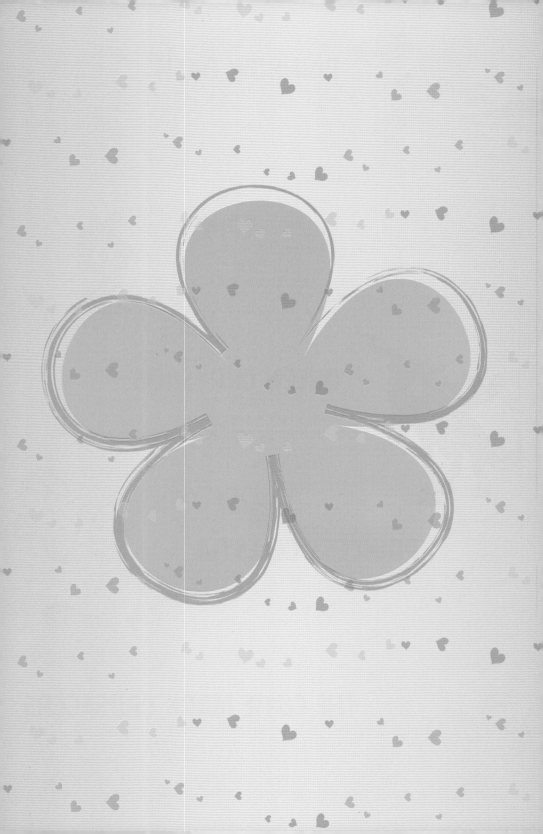

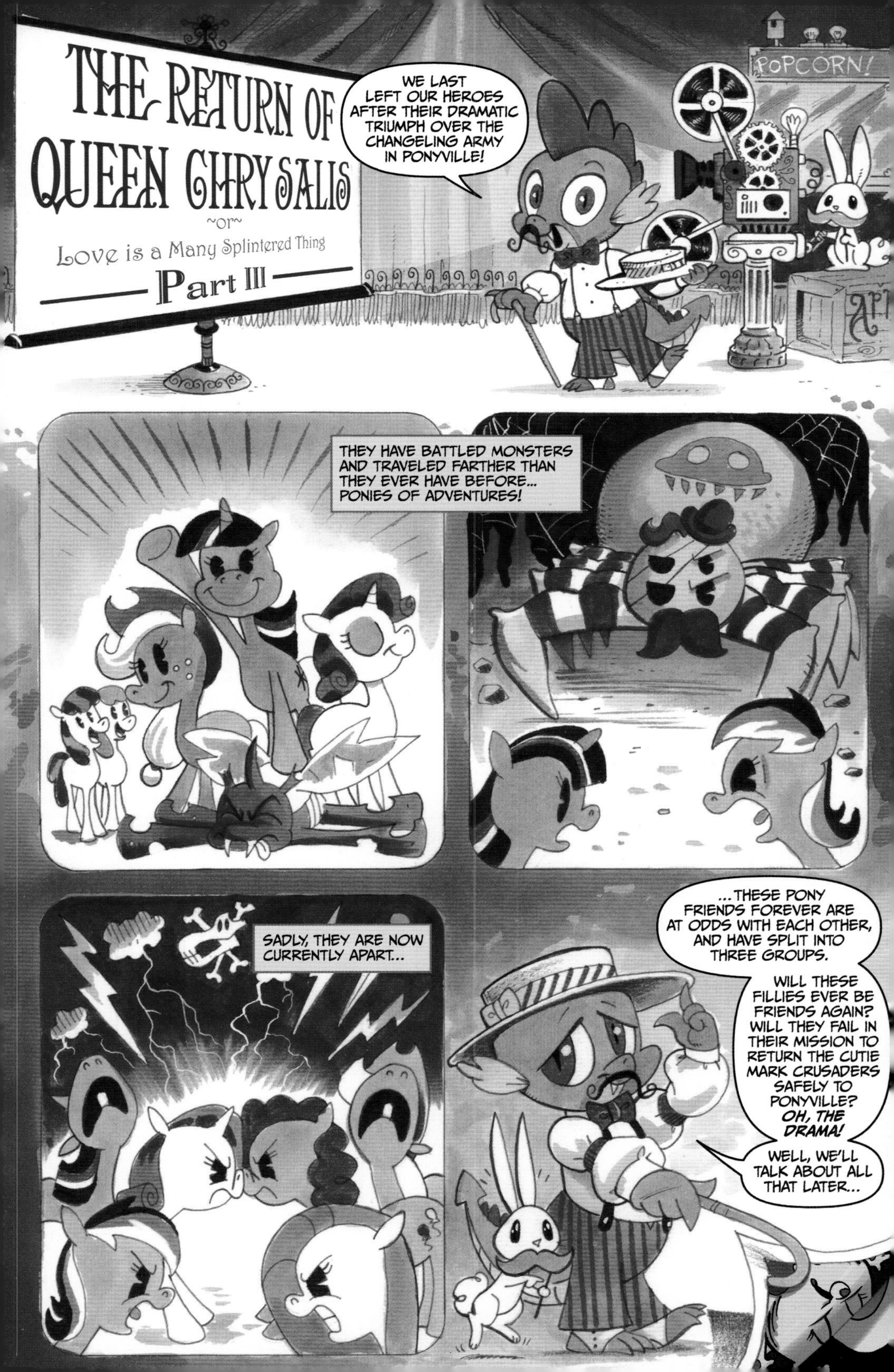
THE RETURN OF QUEEN CHRYSALIS
~or~
Love is a Many Splintered Thing
Part III
WE LAST LEFT OUR HEROES AFTER THEIR DRAMATIC TRIUMPH OVER THE CHANGELING ARMY IN PONYVILLE!
POPCORN!
THEY HAVE BATTLED MONSTERS AND TRAVELED FARTHER THAN THEY EVER HAVE BEFORE... PONIES OF ADVENTURES!
SADLY, THEY ARE NOW CURRENTLY APART...
...THESE PONY FRIENDS FOREVER ARE AT ODDS WITH EACH OTHER, AND HAVE SPLIT INTO THREE GROUPS.
WILL THESE FILLIES EVER BE FRIENDS AGAIN? WILL THEY FAIL IN THEIR MISSION TO RETURN THE CUTIE MARK CRUSADERS SAFELY TO PONYVILLE? *OH, THE DRAMA!*
WELL, WE'LL TALK ABOUT ALL THAT LATER...

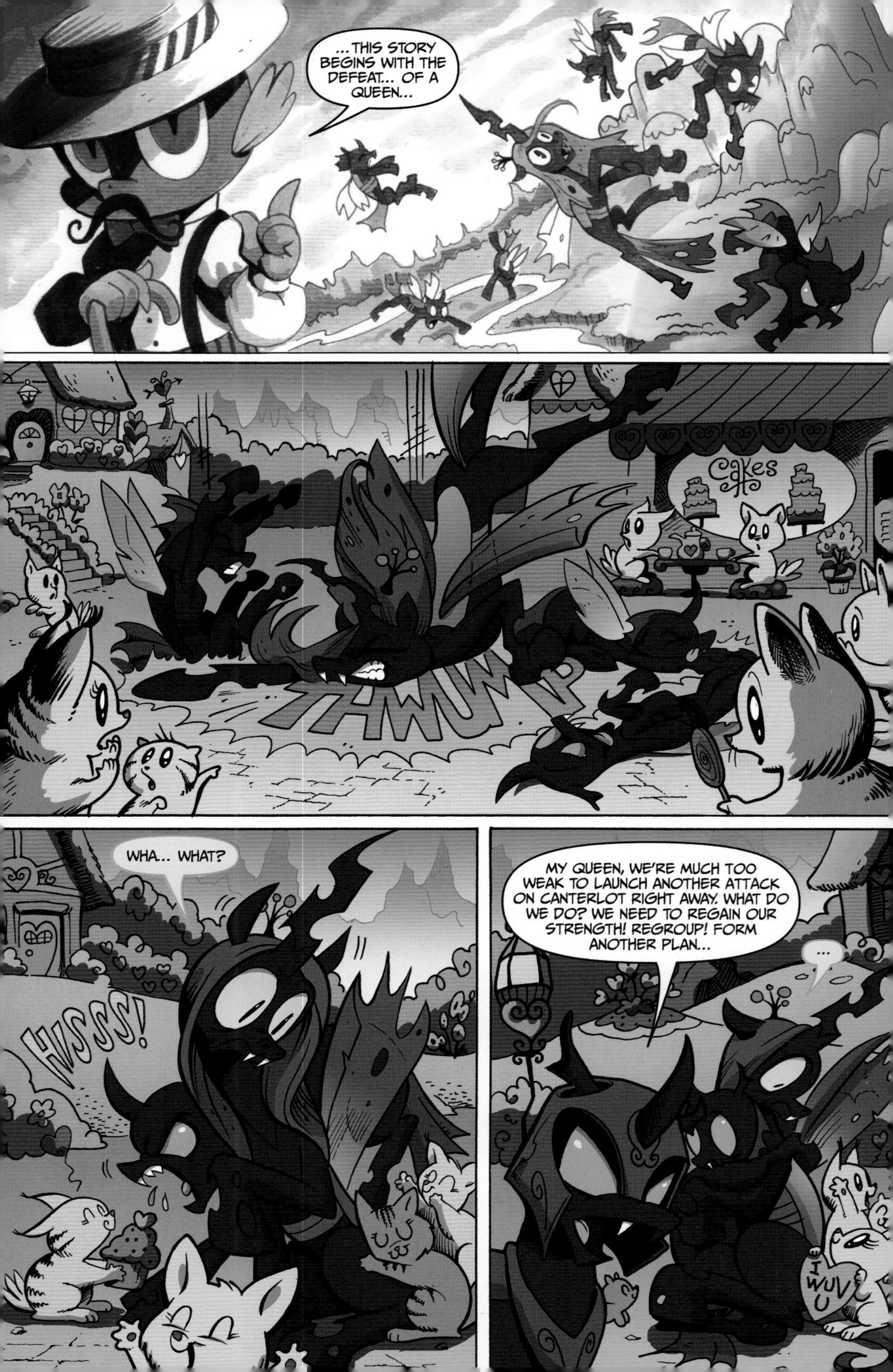
...THIS STORY BEGINS WITH THE DEFEAT... OF A QUEEN...
Cakes
THMUMP
WHA... WHAT?
HSSS!
MY QUEEN, WE'RE MUCH TOO WEAK TO LAUNCH ANOTHER ATTACK ON CANTERLOT RIGHT AWAY. WHAT DO WE DO? WE NEED TO REGAIN OUR STRENGTH! REGROUP! FORM ANOTHER PLAN...
...
I WUV U

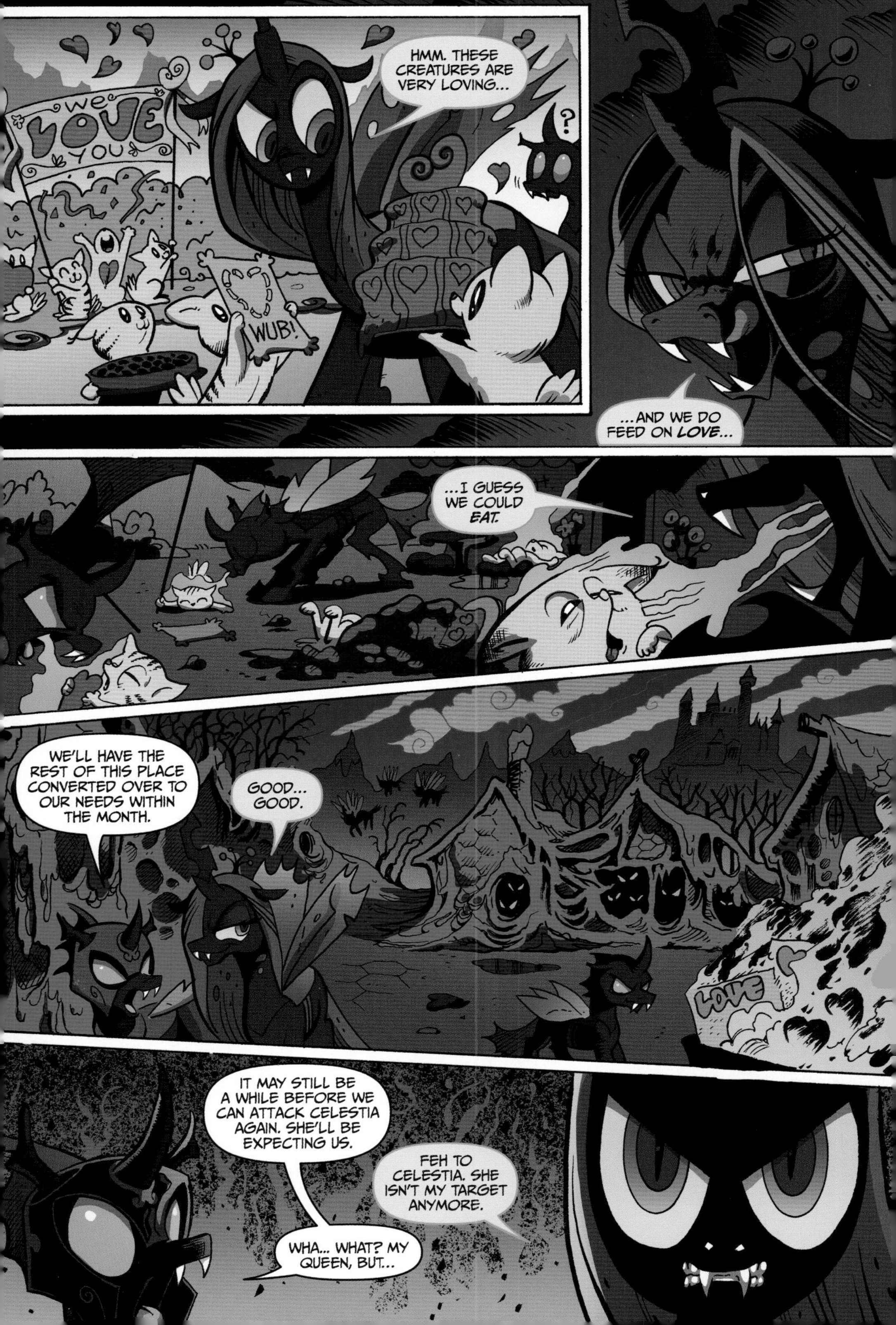
HMM. THESE CREATURES ARE VERY LOVING...
?
WE LOVE YOU
WUB!
...AND WE DO FEED ON LOVE...
...I GUESS WE COULD EAT.
WE'LL HAVE THE REST OF THIS PLACE CONVERTED OVER TO OUR NEEDS WITHIN THE MONTH.
GOOD... GOOD.
LOVE
IT MAY STILL BE A WHILE BEFORE WE CAN ATTACK CELESTIA AGAIN. SHE'LL BE EXPECTING US.
FEH TO CELESTIA. SHE ISN'T MY TARGET ANYMORE.
WHA... WHAT? MY QUEEN, BUT...

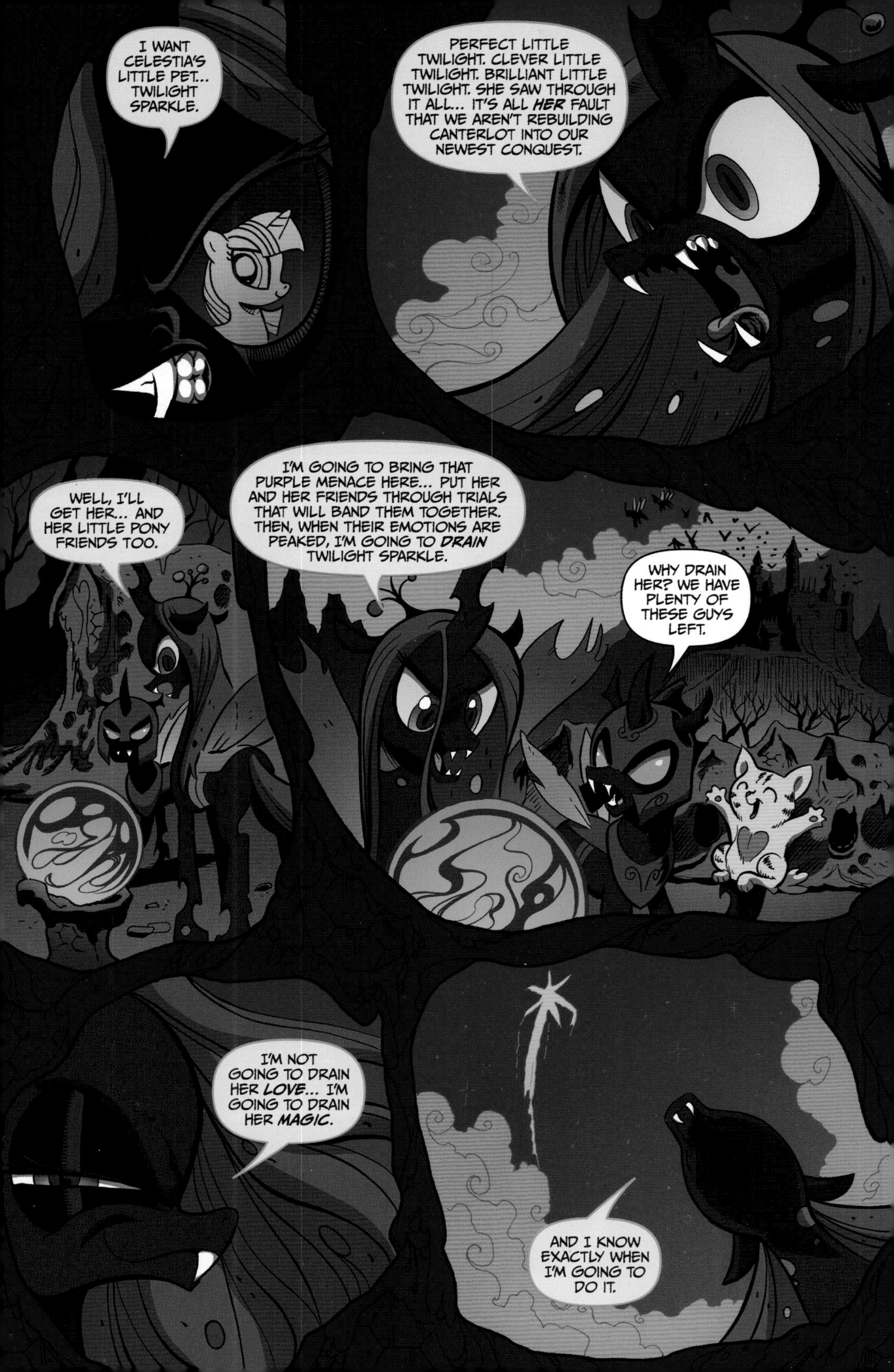
I WANT CELESTIA'S LITTLE PET... TWILIGHT SPARKLE.
PERFECT LITTLE TWILIGHT. CLEVER LITTLE TWILIGHT. BRILLIANT LITTLE TWILIGHT. SHE SAW THROUGH IT ALL... IT'S ALL *HER* FAULT THAT WE AREN'T REBUILDING CANTERLOT INTO OUR NEWEST CONQUEST.
WELL, I'LL GET HER... AND HER LITTLE PONY FRIENDS TOO.
I'M GOING TO BRING THAT PURPLE MENACE HERE... PUT HER AND HER FRIENDS THROUGH TRIALS THAT WILL BAND THEM TOGETHER. THEN, WHEN THEIR EMOTIONS ARE PEAKED, I'M GOING TO *DRAIN* TWILIGHT SPARKLE.
WHY DRAIN HER? WE HAVE PLENTY OF THESE GUYS LEFT.
I'M NOT GOING TO DRAIN HER *LOVE*... I'M GOING TO DRAIN HER *MAGIC*.
AND I KNOW EXACTLY WHEN I'M GOING TO DO IT.

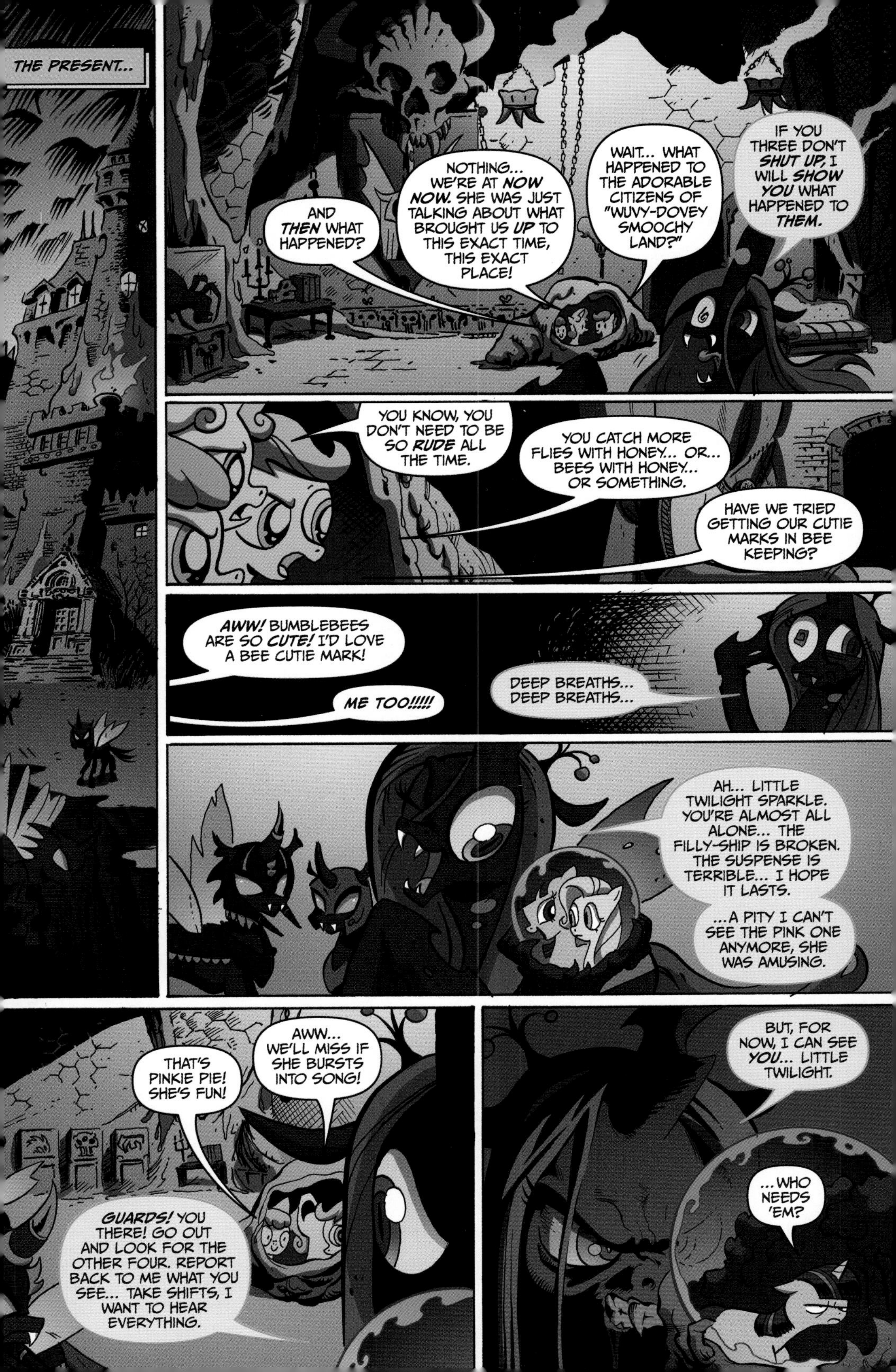
THE PRESENT...
AND THEN WHAT HAPPENED?
NOTHING... WE'RE AT NOW NOW. SHE WAS JUST TALKING ABOUT WHAT BROUGHT US UP TO THIS EXACT TIME, THIS EXACT PLACE!
WAIT... WHAT HAPPENED TO THE ADORABLE CITIZENS OF "WUVY-DOVEY SMOOCHY LAND?"
IF YOU THREE DON'T SHUT UP, I WILL SHOW YOU WHAT HAPPENED TO THEM.
YOU KNOW, YOU DON'T NEED TO BE SO RUDE ALL THE TIME.
YOU CATCH MORE FLIES WITH HONEY... OR... BEES WITH HONEY... OR SOMETHING.
HAVE WE TRIED GETTING OUR CUTIE MARKS IN BEE KEEPING?
AWW! BUMBLEBEES ARE SO CUTE! I'D LOVE A BEE CUTIE MARK!
ME TOO!!!!!
DEEP BREATHS... DEEP BREATHS...
AH... LITTLE TWILIGHT SPARKLE. YOU'RE ALMOST ALL ALONE... THE FILLY-SHIP IS BROKEN. THE SUSPENSE IS TERRIBLE... I HOPE IT LASTS.
...A PITY I CAN'T SEE THE PINK ONE ANYMORE, SHE WAS AMUSING.
THAT'S PINKIE PIE! SHE'S FUN!
AWW... WE'LL MISS IF SHE BURSTS INTO SONG!
GUARDS! YOU THERE! GO OUT AND LOOK FOR THE OTHER FOUR. REPORT BACK TO ME WHAT YOU SEE... TAKE SHIFTS, I WANT TO HEAR EVERYTHING.
BUT, FOR NOW, I CAN SEE YOU... LITTLE TWILIGHT.
...WHO NEEDS 'EM?

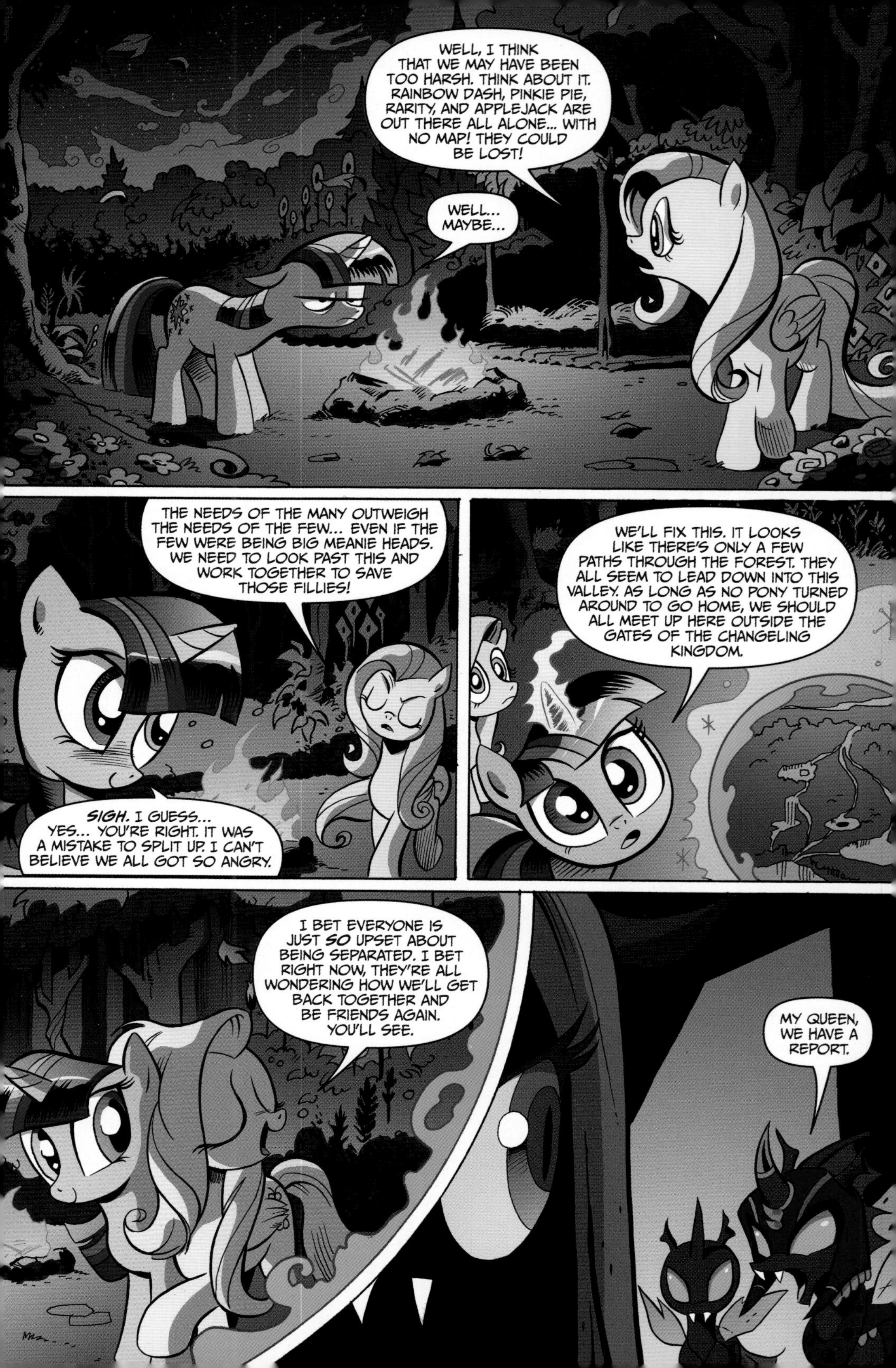
WELL, I THINK THAT WE MAY HAVE BEEN TOO HARSH. THINK ABOUT IT. RAINBOW DASH, PINKIE PIE, RARITY, AND APPLEJACK ARE OUT THERE ALL ALONE... WITH NO MAP! THEY COULD BE LOST!
WELL... MAYBE...
THE NEEDS OF THE MANY OUTWEIGH THE NEEDS OF THE FEW... EVEN IF THE FEW WERE BEING BIG MEANIE HEADS. WE NEED TO LOOK PAST THIS AND WORK TOGETHER TO SAVE THOSE FILLIES!
SIGH. I GUESS... YES... YOU'RE RIGHT. IT WAS A MISTAKE TO SPLIT UP. I CAN'T BELIEVE WE ALL GOT SO ANGRY.
WE'LL FIX THIS. IT LOOKS LIKE THERE'S ONLY A FEW PATHS THROUGH THE FOREST. THEY ALL SEEM TO LEAD DOWN INTO THIS VALLEY. AS LONG AS NO PONY TURNED AROUND TO GO HOME, WE SHOULD ALL MEET UP HERE OUTSIDE THE GATES OF THE CHANGELING KINGDOM.
I BET EVERYONE IS JUST SO UPSET ABOUT BEING SEPARATED. I BET RIGHT NOW, THEY'RE ALL WONDERING HOW WE'LL GET BACK TOGETHER AND BE FRIENDS AGAIN. YOU'LL SEE.
MY QUEEN, WE HAVE A REPORT.

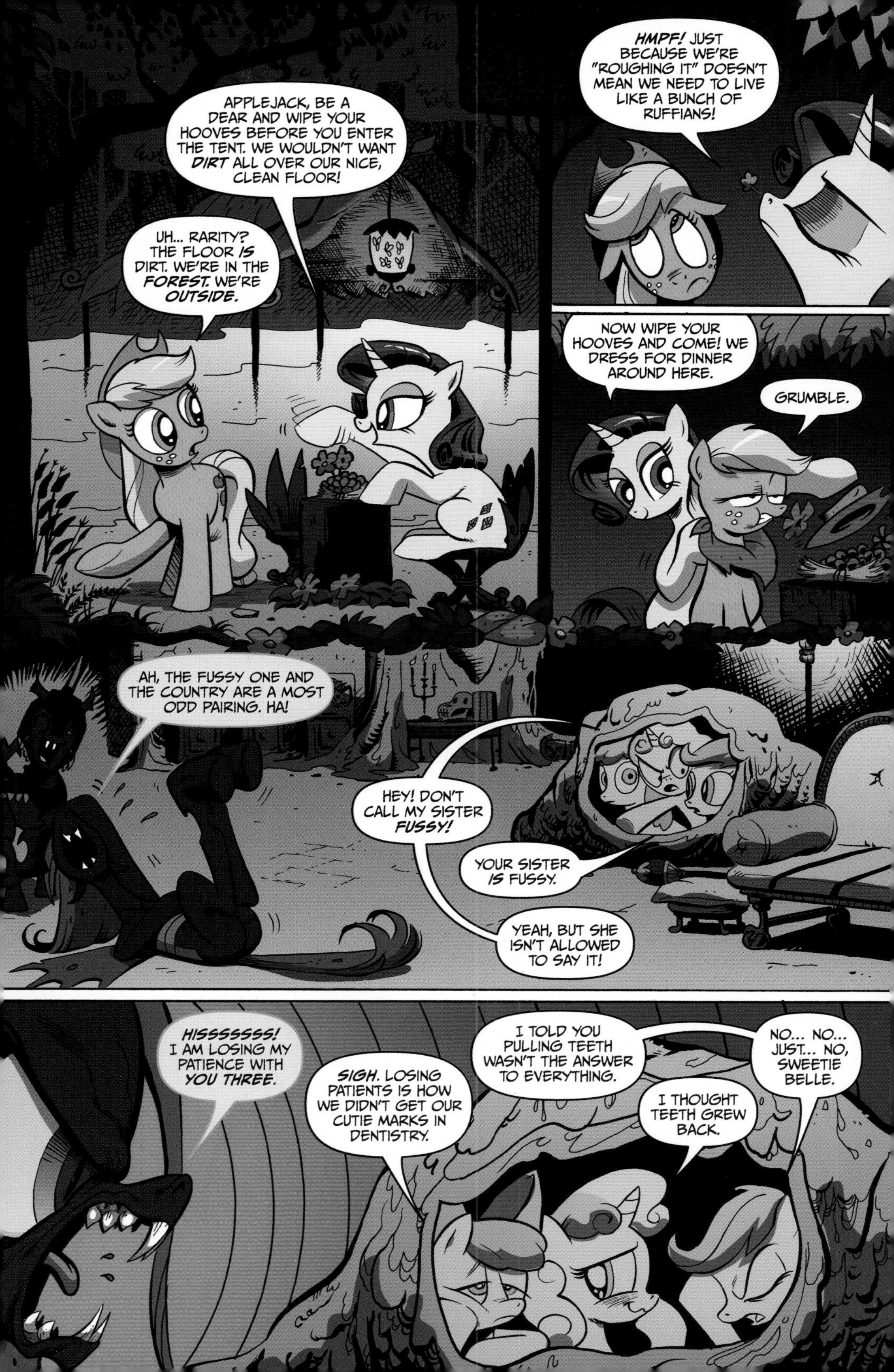
APPLEJACK, BE A DEAR AND WIPE YOUR HOOVES BEFORE YOU ENTER THE TENT. WE WOULDN'T WANT DIRT ALL OVER OUR NICE, CLEAN FLOOR!
UH... RARITY? THE FLOOR IS DIRT. WE'RE IN THE FOREST. WE'RE OUTSIDE.
HMPF! JUST BECAUSE WE'RE "ROUGHING IT" DOESN'T MEAN WE NEED TO LIVE LIKE A BUNCH OF RUFFIANS!
NOW WIPE YOUR HOOVES AND COME! WE DRESS FOR DINNER AROUND HERE.
GRUMBLE.
AH, THE FUSSY ONE AND THE COUNTRY ARE A MOST ODD PAIRING. HA!
HEY! DON'T CALL MY SISTER FUSSY!
YOUR SISTER IS FUSSY.
YEAH, BUT SHE ISN'T ALLOWED TO SAY IT!
HISSSSSSS! I AM LOSING MY PATIENCE WITH YOU THREE.
SIGH. LOSING PATIENTS IS HOW WE DIDN'T GET OUR CUTIE MARKS IN DENTISTRY.
I TOLD YOU PULLING TEETH WASN'T THE ANSWER TO EVERYTHING.
I THOUGHT TEETH GREW BACK.
NO... NO... JUST... NO, SWEETIE BELLE.

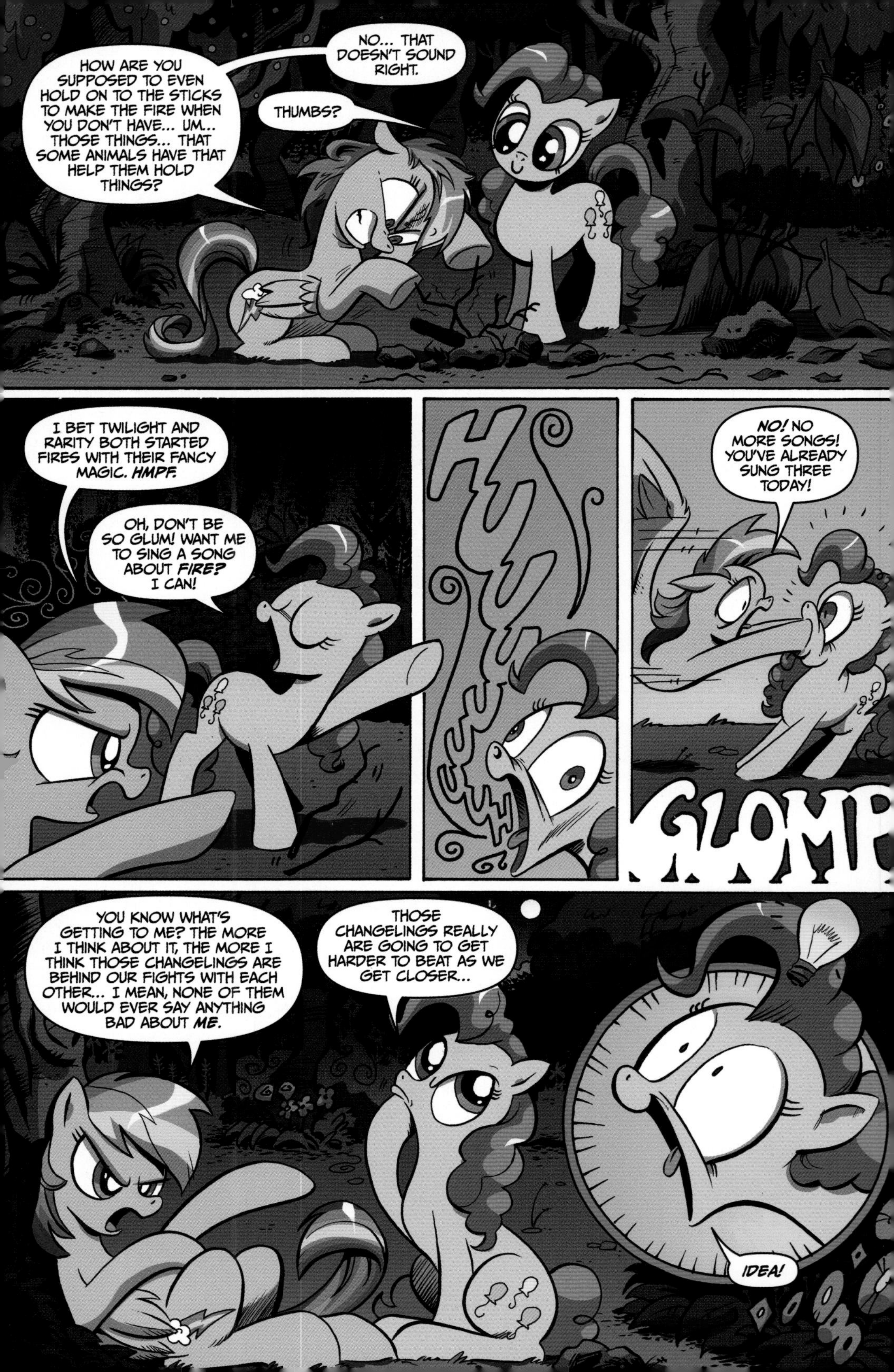
HOW ARE YOU SUPPOSED TO EVEN HOLD ON TO THE STICKS TO MAKE THE FIRE WHEN YOU DON'T HAVE... UM... THOSE THINGS... THAT SOME ANIMALS HAVE THAT HELP THEM HOLD THINGS?
THUMBS?
NO... THAT DOESN'T SOUND RIGHT.
I BET TWILIGHT AND RARITY BOTH STARTED FIRES WITH THEIR FANCY MAGIC. HMPF.
OH, DON'T BE SO GLUM! WANT ME TO SING A SONG ABOUT FIRE? I CAN!
HUUUUH
NO! NO MORE SONGS! YOU'VE ALREADY SUNG THREE TODAY!
GLOMP
YOU KNOW WHAT'S GETTING TO ME? THE MORE I THINK ABOUT IT, THE MORE I THINK THOSE CHANGELINGS ARE BEHIND OUR FIGHTS WITH EACH OTHER... I MEAN, NONE OF THEM WOULD EVER SAY ANYTHING BAD ABOUT ME.
THOSE CHANGELINGS REALLY ARE GOING TO GET HARDER TO BEAT AS WE GET CLOSER...
IDEA!

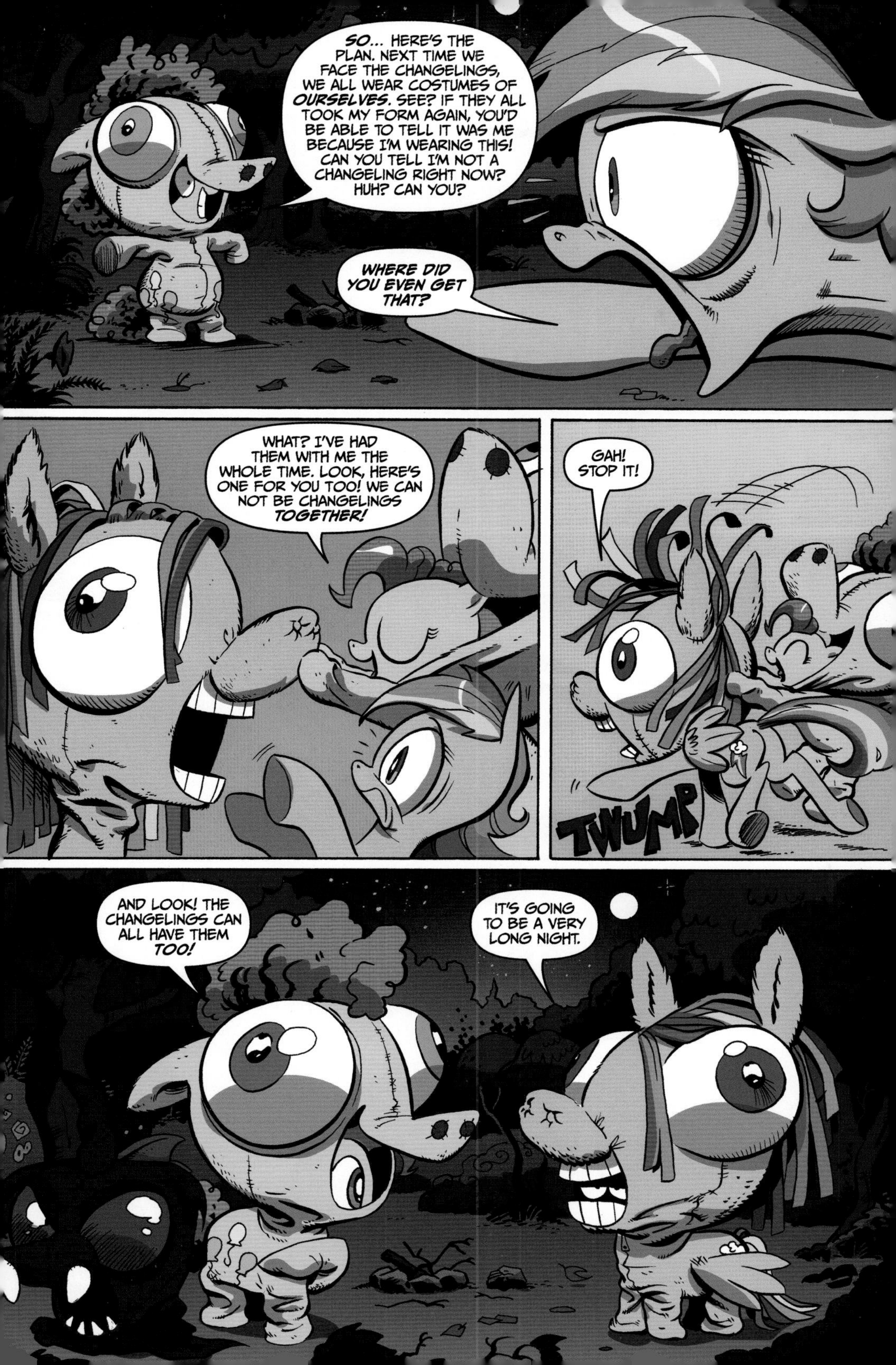
SO... HERE'S THE PLAN. NEXT TIME WE FACE THE CHANGELINGS, WE ALL WEAR COSTUMES OF OURSELVES. SEE? IF THEY ALL TOOK MY FORM AGAIN, YOU'D BE ABLE TO TELL IT WAS ME BECAUSE I'M WEARING THIS! CAN YOU TELL I'M NOT A CHANGELING RIGHT NOW? HUH? CAN YOU?
WHERE DID YOU EVEN GET THAT?
WHAT? I'VE HAD THEM WITH ME THE WHOLE TIME. LOOK, HERE'S ONE FOR YOU TOO! WE CAN NOT BE CHANGELINGS TOGETHER!
GAH! STOP IT!
TWUMP
AND LOOK! THE CHANGELINGS CAN ALL HAVE THEM TOO!
IT'S GOING TO BE A VERY LONG NIGHT.

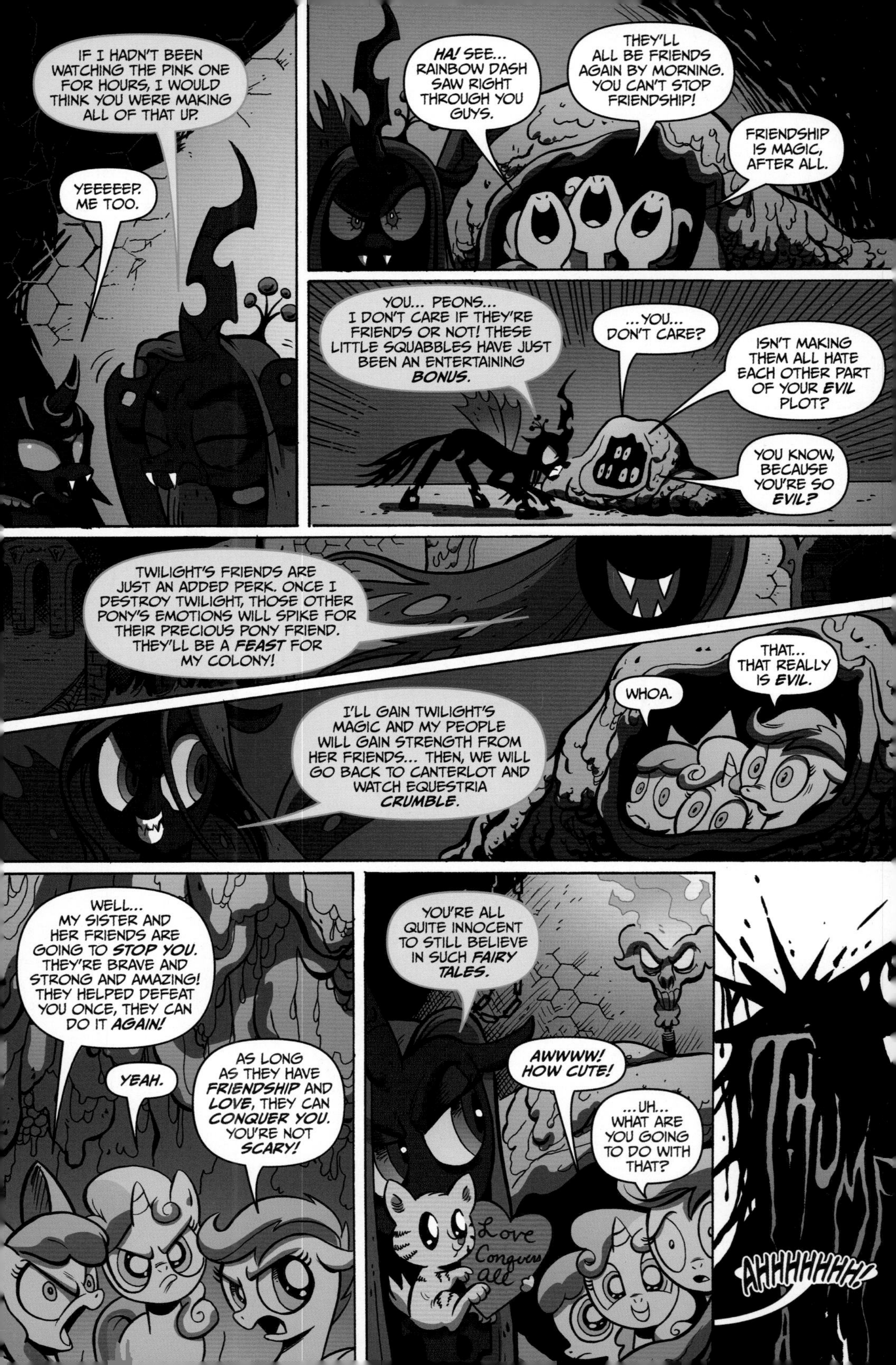
IF I HADN'T BEEN WATCHING THE PINK ONE FOR HOURS, I WOULD THINK YOU WERE MAKING ALL OF THAT UP.
YEEEEEP. ME TOO.
HA! SEE... RAINBOW DASH SAW RIGHT THROUGH YOU GUYS.
THEY'LL ALL BE FRIENDS AGAIN BY MORNING. YOU CAN'T STOP FRIENDSHIP!
FRIENDSHIP IS MAGIC, AFTER ALL.
YOU... PEONS... I DON'T CARE IF THEY'RE FRIENDS OR NOT! THESE LITTLE SQUABBLES HAVE JUST BEEN AN ENTERTAINING BONUS.
...YOU... DON'T CARE?
ISN'T MAKING THEM ALL HATE EACH OTHER PART OF YOUR EVIL PLOT?
YOU KNOW, BECAUSE YOU'RE SO EVIL?
TWILIGHT'S FRIENDS ARE JUST AN ADDED PERK. ONCE I DESTROY TWILIGHT, THOSE OTHER PONY'S EMOTIONS WILL SPIKE FOR THEIR PRECIOUS PONY FRIEND. THEY'LL BE A FEAST FOR MY COLONY!
I'LL GAIN TWILIGHT'S MAGIC AND MY PEOPLE WILL GAIN STRENGTH FROM HER FRIENDS... THEN, WE WILL GO BACK TO CANTERLOT AND WATCH EQUESTRIA CRUMBLE.
WHOA.
THAT... THAT REALLY IS EVIL.
WELL... MY SISTER AND HER FRIENDS ARE GOING TO STOP YOU. THEY'RE BRAVE AND STRONG AND AMAZING! THEY HELPED DEFEAT YOU ONCE, THEY CAN DO IT AGAIN!
YEAH.
AS LONG AS THEY HAVE FRIENDSHIP AND LOVE, THEY CAN CONQUER YOU. YOU'RE NOT SCARY!
YOU'RE ALL QUITE INNOCENT TO STILL BELIEVE IN SUCH FAIRY TALES.
AWWWW! HOW CUTE!
...UH... WHAT ARE YOU GOING TO DO WITH THAT?
Love Conquers All
AHHHHHHH!

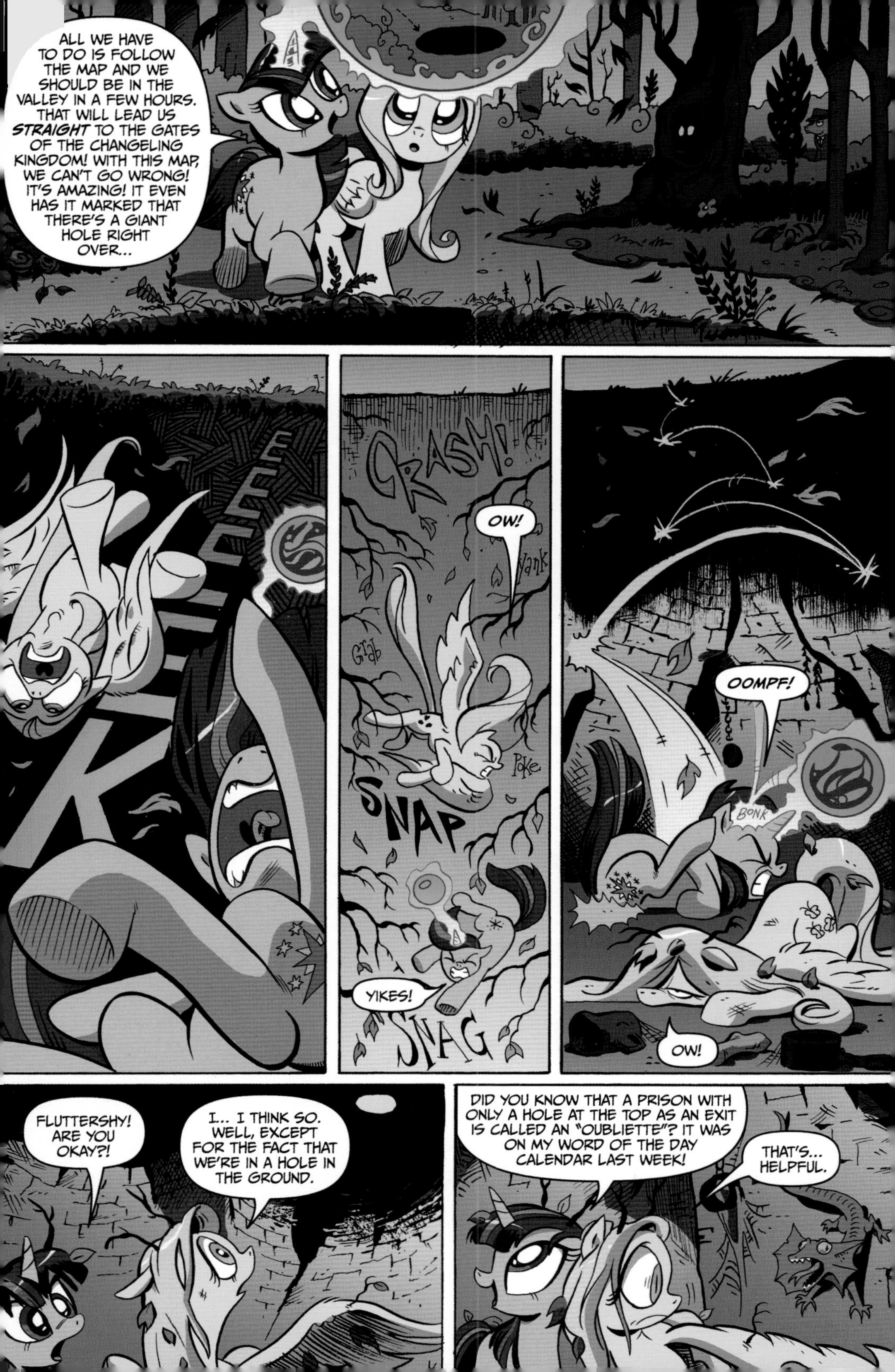
ALL WE HAVE TO DO IS FOLLOW THE MAP AND WE SHOULD BE IN THE VALLEY IN A FEW HOURS. THAT WILL LEAD US **STRAIGHT** TO THE GATES OF THE CHANGELING KINGDOM! WITH THIS MAP, WE CAN'T GO WRONG! IT'S AMAZING! IT EVEN HAS IT MARKED THAT THERE'S A GIANT HOLE RIGHT OVER...
CRASH!
OW!
yank
Grab
Poke
SNAP
YIKES!
SNAG
OOMPF!
BONK
OW!
FLUTTERSHY! ARE YOU OKAY?!
I... I THINK SO. WELL, EXCEPT FOR THE FACT THAT WE'RE IN A HOLE IN THE GROUND.
DID YOU KNOW THAT A PRISON WITH ONLY A HOLE AT THE TOP AS AN EXIT IS CALLED AN "OUBLIETTE"? IT WAS ON MY WORD OF THE DAY CALENDAR LAST WEEK!
THAT'S... HELPFUL.

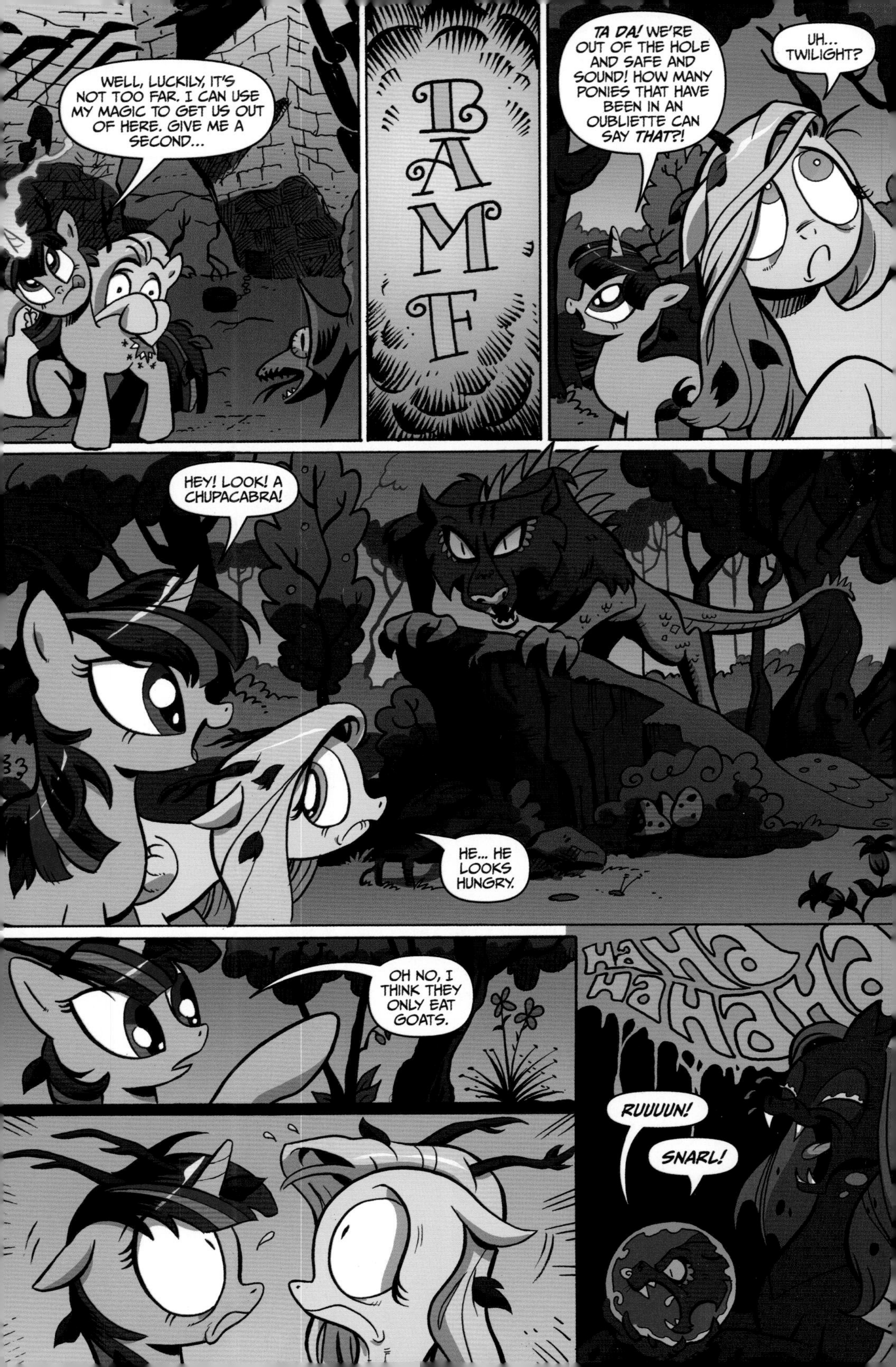
WELL, LUCKILY, IT'S NOT TOO FAR. I CAN USE MY MAGIC TO GET US OUT OF HERE. GIVE ME A SECOND...
BAMF
TA DA! WE'RE OUT OF THE HOLE AND SAFE AND SOUND! HOW MANY PONIES THAT HAVE BEEN IN AN OUBLIETTE CAN SAY THAT?!
UH... TWILIGHT?
HEY! LOOK! A CHUPACABRA!
HE... HE LOOKS HUNGRY.
OH NO, I THINK THEY ONLY EAT GOATS.
RUUUUN!
SNARL!

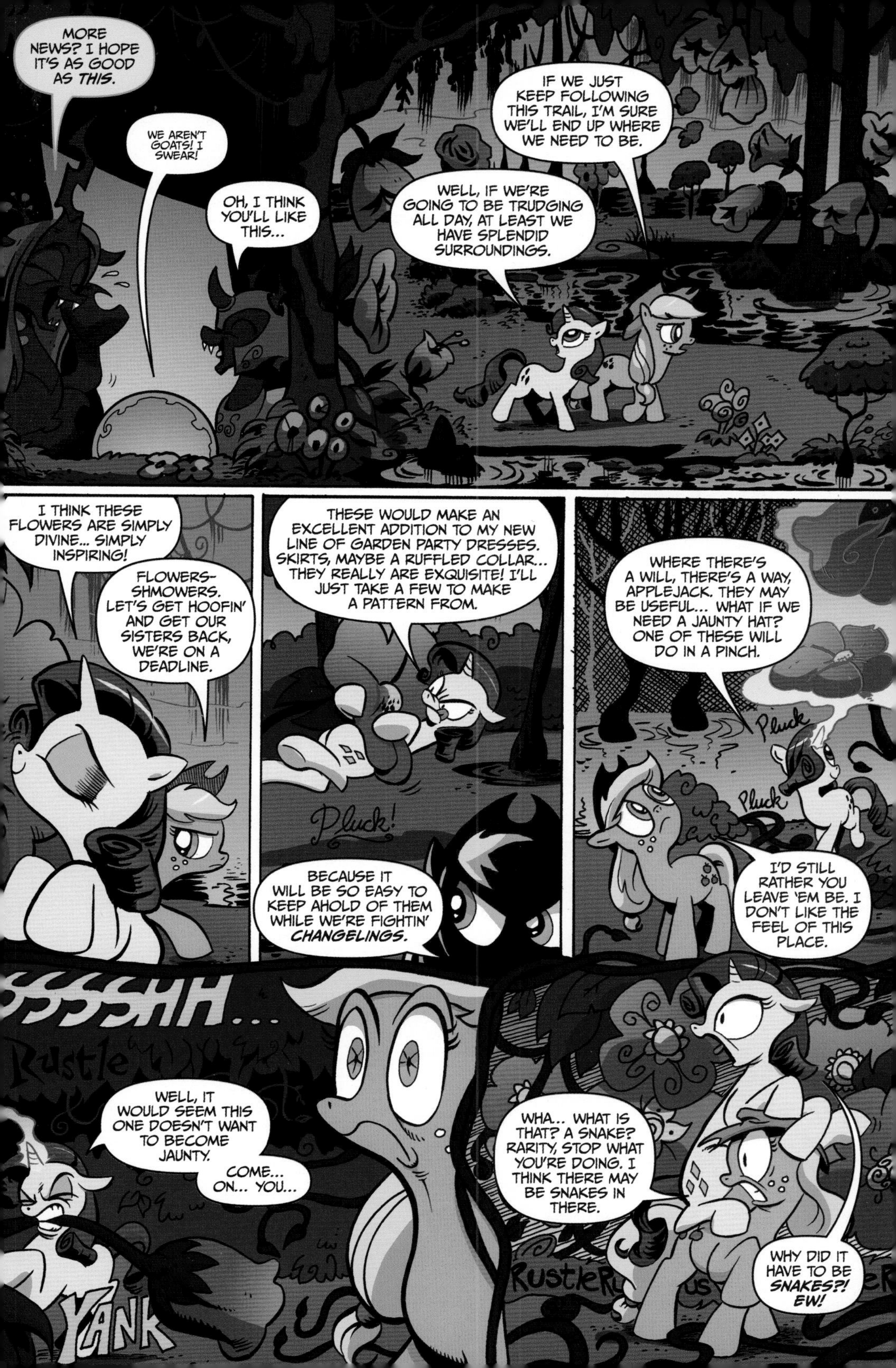

MORE NEWS? I HOPE IT'S AS GOOD AS *THIS*.
WE AREN'T GOATS! I SWEAR!
OH, I THINK YOU'LL LIKE THIS...
IF WE JUST KEEP FOLLOWING THIS TRAIL, I'M SURE WE'LL END UP WHERE WE NEED TO BE.
WELL, IF WE'RE GOING TO BE TRUDGING ALL DAY, AT LEAST WE HAVE SPLENDID SURROUNDINGS.
I THINK THESE FLOWERS ARE SIMPLY DIVINE... SIMPLY INSPIRING!
FLOWERS-SHMOWERS. LET'S GET HOOFIN' AND GET OUR SISTERS BACK, WE'RE ON A DEADLINE.
THESE WOULD MAKE AN EXCELLENT ADDITION TO MY NEW LINE OF GARDEN PARTY DRESSES. SKIRTS, MAYBE A RUFFLED COLLAR... THEY REALLY ARE EXQUISITE! I'LL JUST TAKE A FEW TO MAKE A PATTERN FROM.
Pluck!
BECAUSE IT WILL BE SO EASY TO KEEP AHOLD OF THEM WHILE WE'RE FIGHTIN' *CHANGELINGS.*
WHERE THERE'S A WILL, THERE'S A WAY, APPLEJACK. THEY MAY BE USEFUL... WHAT IF WE NEED A JAUNTY HAT? ONE OF THESE WILL DO IN A PINCH.
Pluck
Pluck
I'D STILL RATHER YOU LEAVE 'EM BE. I DON'T LIKE THE FEEL OF THIS PLACE.
SSSSHH...
Rustle
WELL, IT WOULD SEEM THIS ONE DOESN'T WANT TO BECOME JAUNTY.
COME... ON... YOU...
YANK
WHA... WHAT IS THAT? A SNAKE? RARITY, STOP WHAT YOU'RE DOING. I THINK THERE MAY BE SNAKES IN THERE.
WHY DID IT HAVE TO BE *SNAKES?!* *EW!*

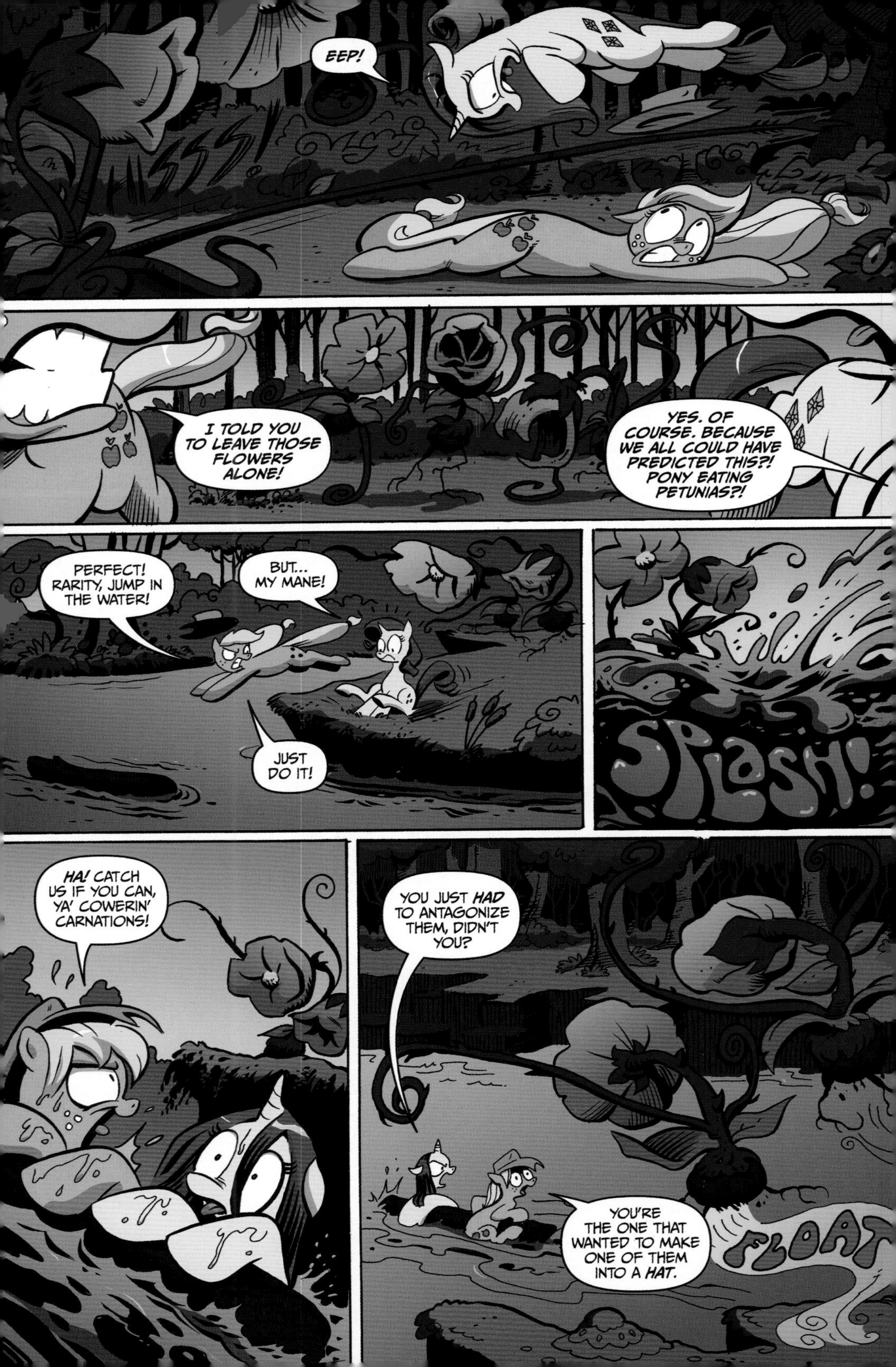
EEP!
HISSSS!
I TOLD YOU TO LEAVE THOSE FLOWERS ALONE!
YES. OF COURSE. BECAUSE WE ALL COULD HAVE PREDICTED THIS?! PONY EATING PETUNIAS?!
PERFECT! RARITY, JUMP IN THE WATER!
BUT... MY MANE!
JUST DO IT!
SPLASH!
HA! CATCH US IF YOU CAN, YA' COWERIN' CARNATIONS!
YOU JUST HAD TO ANTAGONIZE THEM, DIDN'T YOU?
YOU'RE THE ONE THAT WANTED TO MAKE ONE OF THEM INTO A HAT.
FLOAT

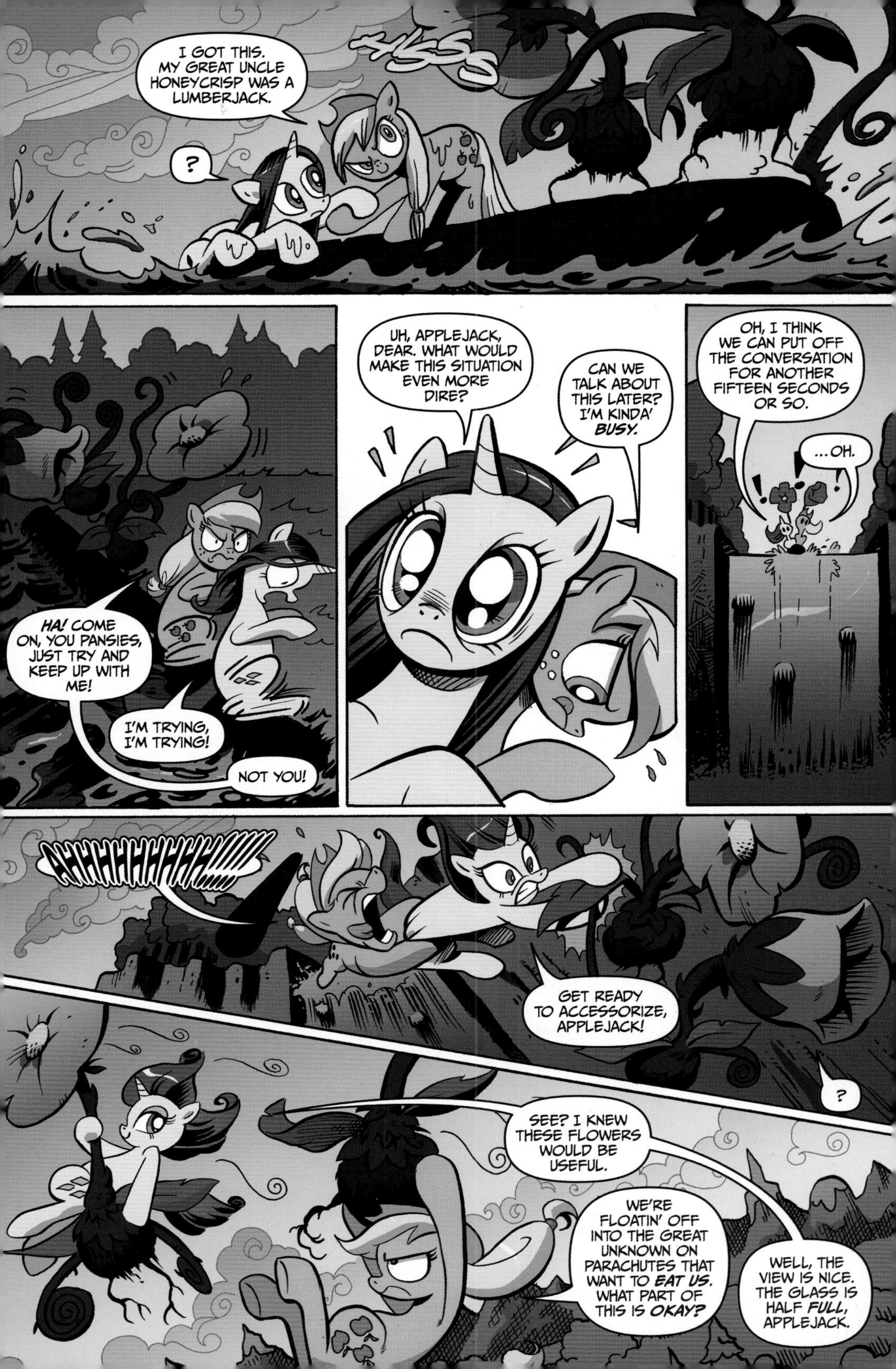
I GOT THIS. MY GREAT UNCLE HONEYCRISP WAS A LUMBERJACK.
HISSS
?
HA! COME ON, YOU PANSIES, JUST TRY AND KEEP UP WITH ME!
I'M TRYING, I'M TRYING!
NOT YOU!
UH, APPLEJACK, DEAR. WHAT WOULD MAKE THIS SITUATION EVEN MORE DIRE?
CAN WE TALK ABOUT THIS LATER? I'M KINDA' BUSY.
OH, I THINK WE CAN PUT OFF THE CONVERSATION FOR ANOTHER FIFTEEN SECONDS OR SO.
...OH.
AHHHHHHHHH!!!!!
GET READY TO ACCESSORIZE, APPLEJACK!
?
SEE? I KNEW THESE FLOWERS WOULD BE USEFUL.
WE'RE FLOATIN' OFF INTO THE GREAT UNKNOWN ON PARACHUTES THAT WANT TO EAT US. WHAT PART OF THIS IS OKAY?
WELL, THE VIEW IS NICE. THE GLASS IS HALF FULL, APPLEJACK.

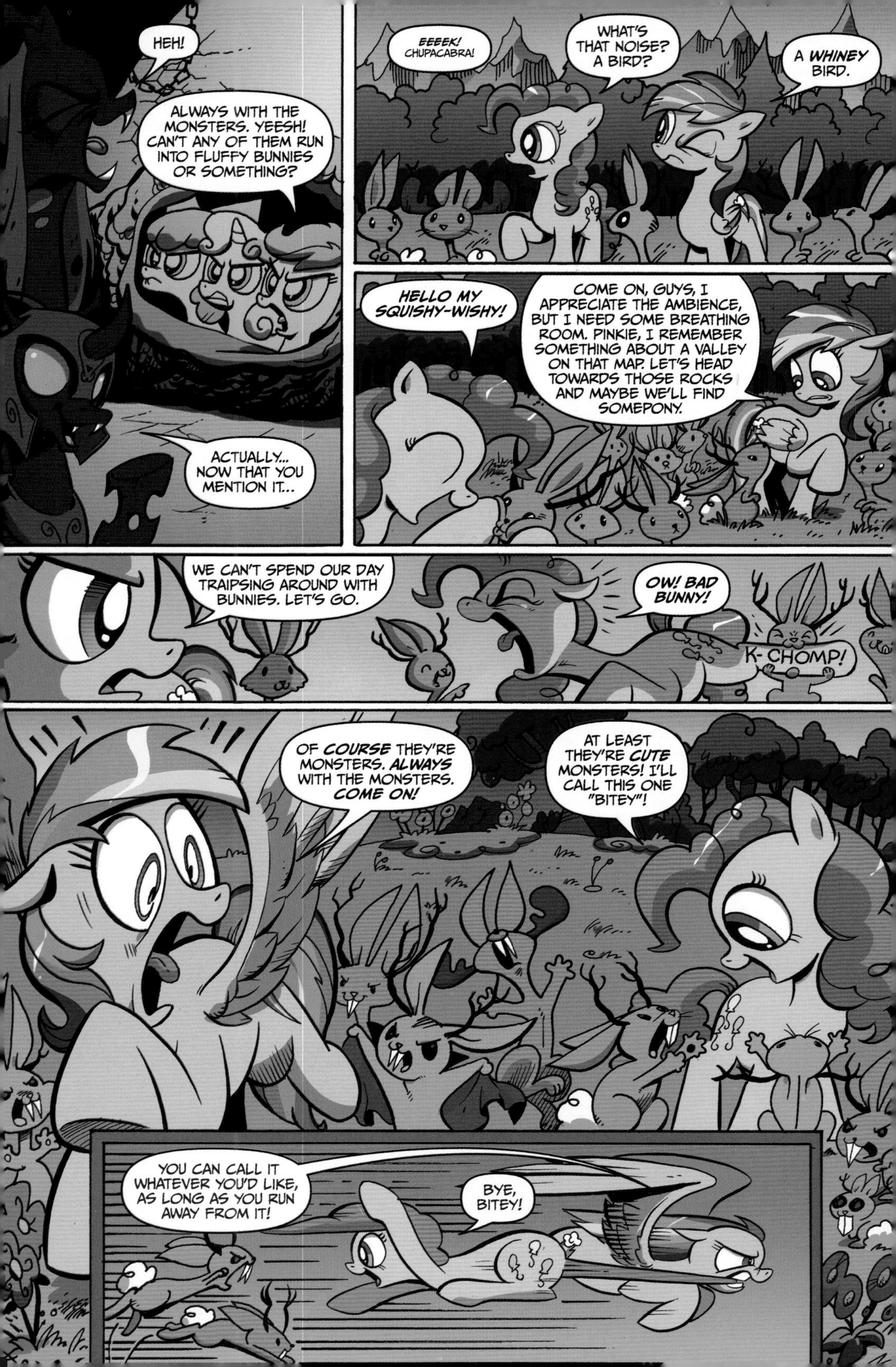
HEH!
ALWAYS WITH THE MONSTERS. YEESH! CAN'T ANY OF THEM RUN INTO FLUFFY BUNNIES OR SOMETHING?
ACTUALLY... NOW THAT YOU MENTION IT...
EEEEK! CHUPACABRA!
WHAT'S THAT NOISE? A BIRD?
A WHINEY BIRD.
HELLO MY SQUISHY-WISHY!
COME ON, GUYS, I APPRECIATE THE AMBIENCE, BUT I NEED SOME BREATHING ROOM. PINKIE, I REMEMBER SOMETHING ABOUT A VALLEY ON THAT MAP. LET'S HEAD TOWARDS THOSE ROCKS AND MAYBE WE'LL FIND SOMEPONY.
WE CAN'T SPEND OUR DAY TRAIPSING AROUND WITH BUNNIES. LET'S GO.
OW! BAD BUNNY!
K-CHOMP!
OF COURSE THEY'RE MONSTERS. ALWAYS WITH THE MONSTERS. COME ON!
AT LEAST THEY'RE CUTE MONSTERS! I'LL CALL THIS ONE "BITEY"!
YOU CAN CALL IT WHATEVER YOU'D LIKE, AS LONG AS YOU RUN AWAY FROM IT!
BYE, BITEY!

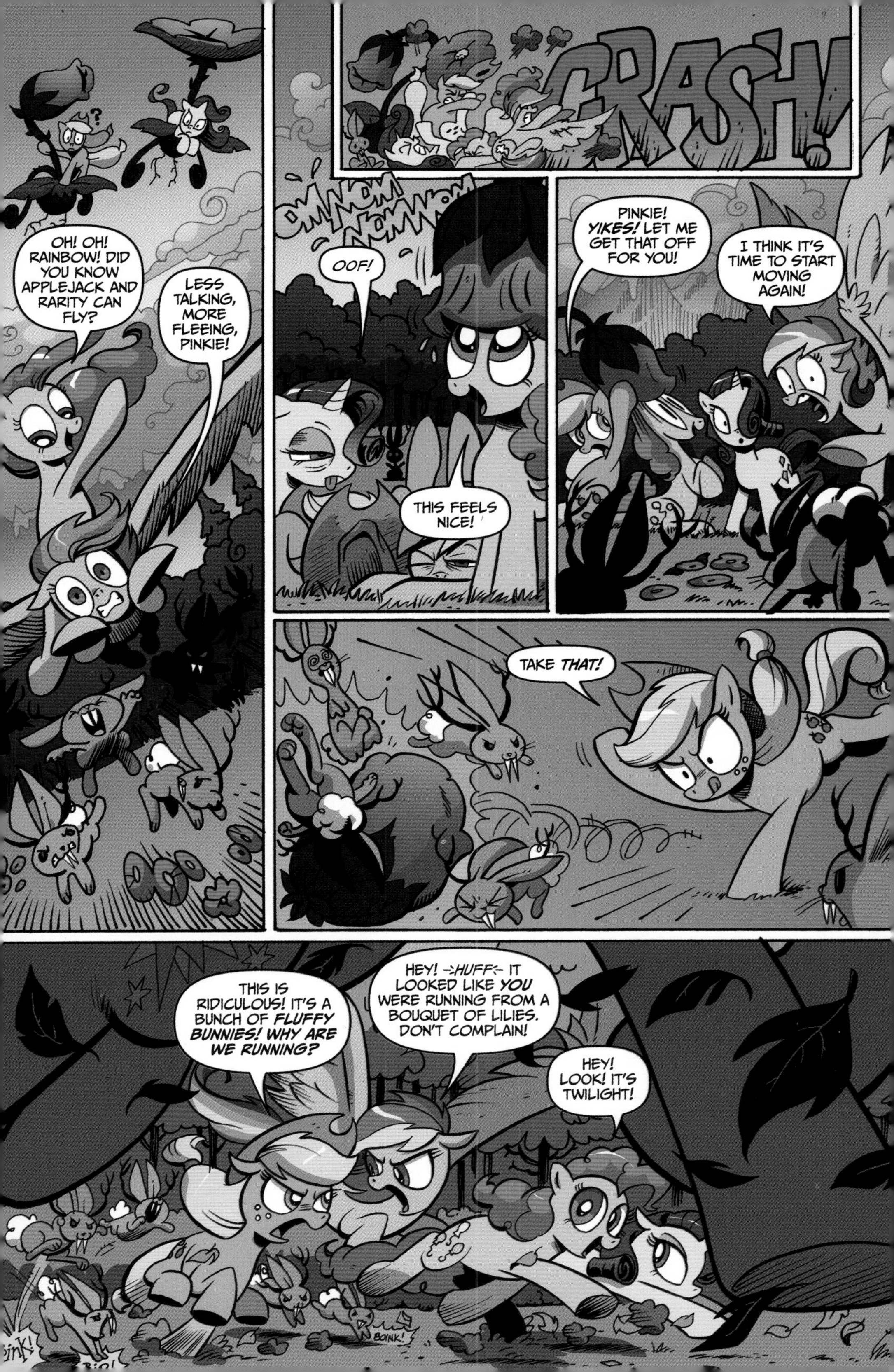
OH! OH! RAINBOW! DID YOU KNOW APPLEJACK AND RARITY CAN FLY?
LESS TALKING, MORE FLEEING, PINKIE!
CRASH!
OM NOM NOM NOM NOM
OOF!
THIS FEELS NICE!
PINKIE! YIKES! LET ME GET THAT OFF FOR YOU!
I THINK IT'S TIME TO START MOVING AGAIN!
TAKE THAT!
THIS IS RIDICULOUS! IT'S A BUNCH OF FLUFFY BUNNIES! WHY ARE WE RUNNING?
HEY! ⇒HUFF⇐ IT LOOKED LIKE YOU WERE RUNNING FROM A BOUQUET OF LILIES. DON'T COMPLAIN!
HEY! LOOK! IT'S TWILIGHT!
BOINK!

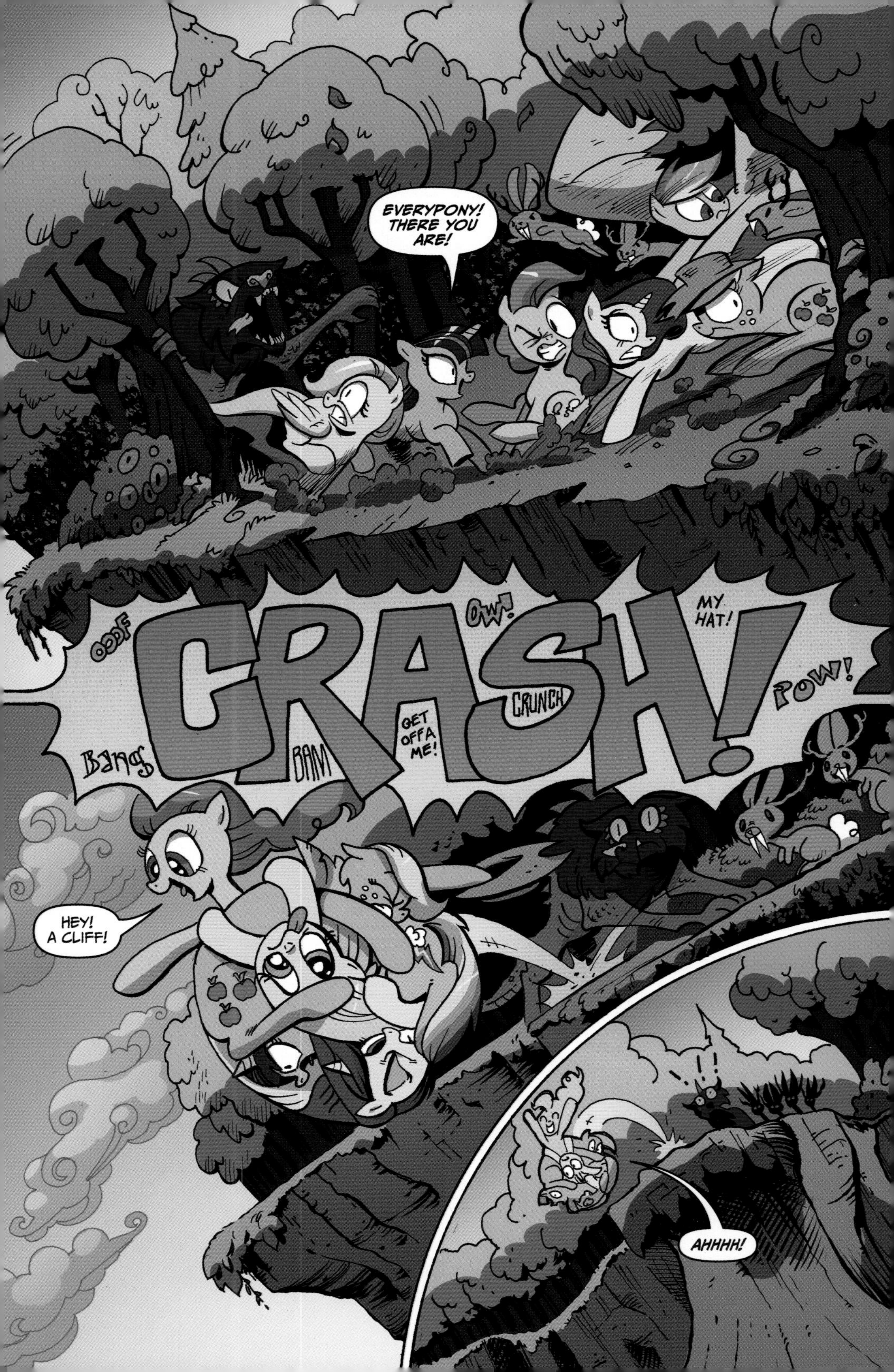
EVERYPONY! THERE YOU ARE!
OOOF
OW!
MY HAT!
CRASH!
CRUNCH
POW!
GET OFFA ME!
BANG
BAM
HEY! A CLIFF!
!!
AHHHH!

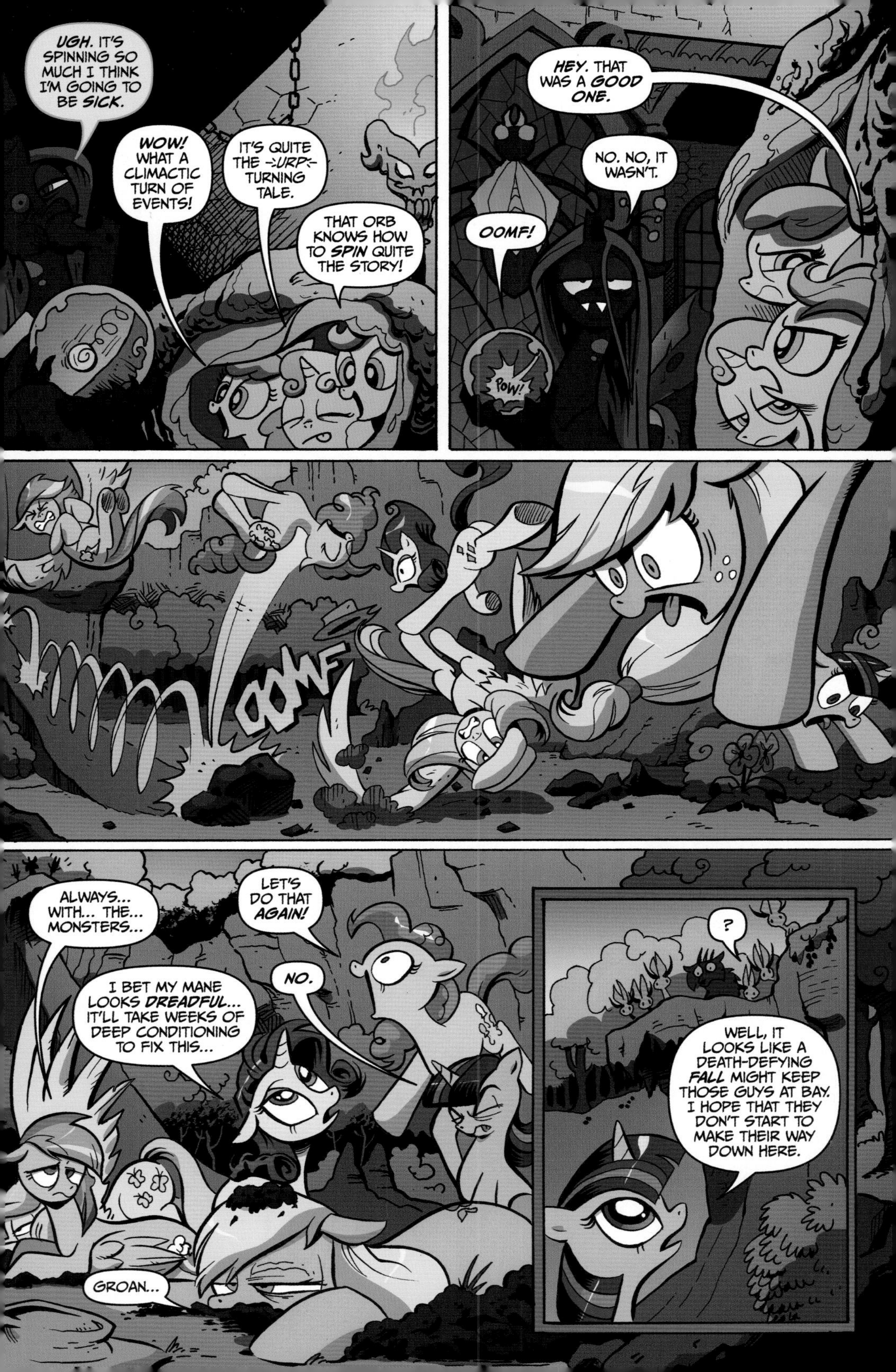
UGH. IT'S SPINNING SO MUCH I THINK I'M GOING TO BE SICK.
WOW! WHAT A CLIMACTIC TURN OF EVENTS!
IT'S QUITE THE -URP- TURNING TALE.
THAT ORB KNOWS HOW TO SPIN QUITE THE STORY!
HEY. THAT WAS A GOOD ONE.
NO. NO, IT WASN'T.
OOMF!
POW!
OOMF
ALWAYS... WITH... THE... MONSTERS...
LET'S DO THAT AGAIN!
I BET MY MANE LOOKS DREADFUL... IT'LL TAKE WEEKS OF DEEP CONDITIONING TO FIX THIS...
NO.
GROAN...
?
WELL, IT LOOKS LIKE A DEATH-DEFYING FALL MIGHT KEEP THOSE GUYS AT BAY. I HOPE THAT THEY DON'T START TO MAKE THEIR WAY DOWN HERE.

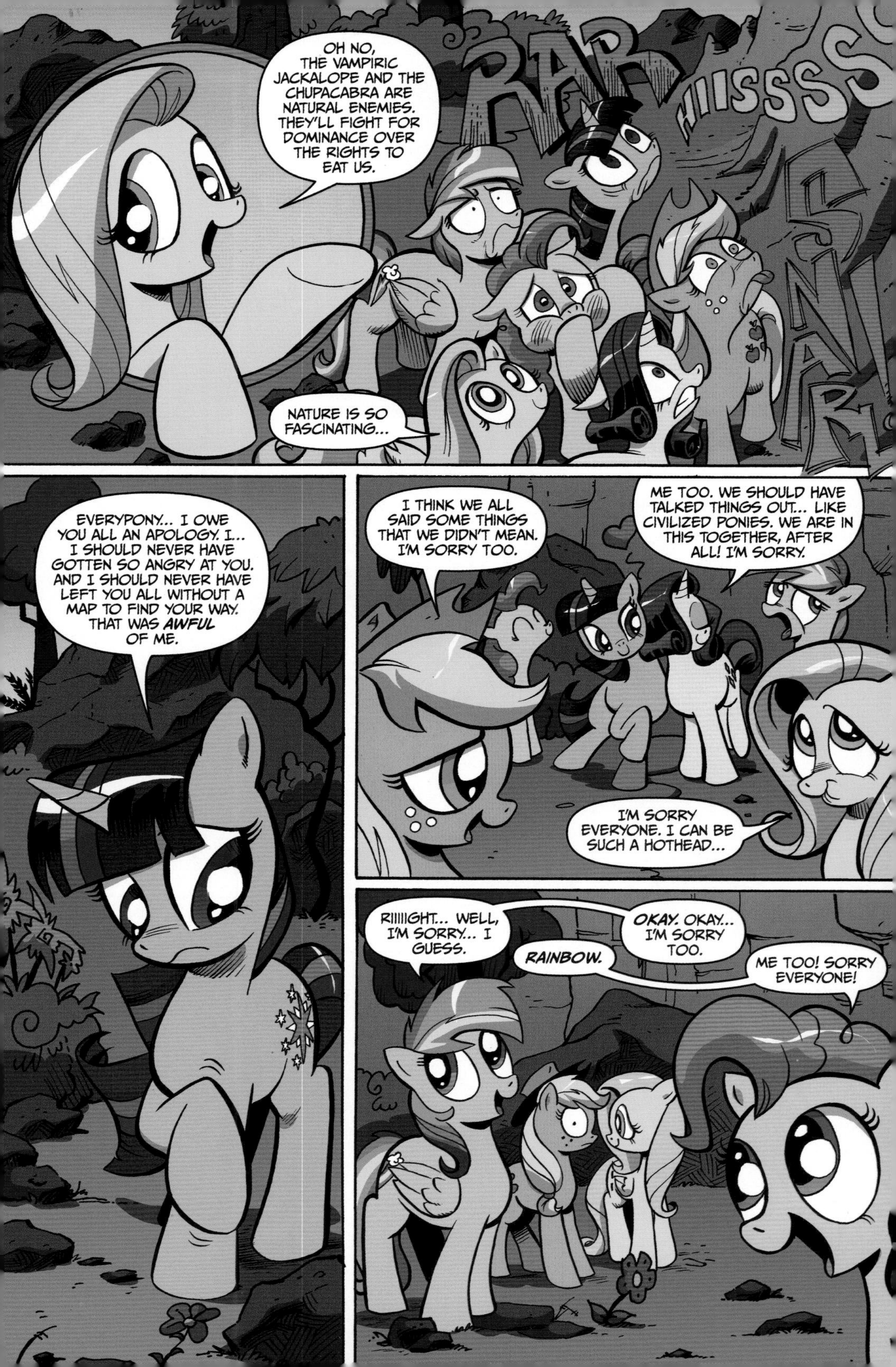
OH NO, THE VAMPIRIC JACKALOPE AND THE CHUPACABRA ARE NATURAL ENEMIES. THEY'LL FIGHT FOR DOMINANCE OVER THE RIGHTS TO EAT US.
RAR
NATURE IS SO FASCINATING...
EVERYPONY... I OWE YOU ALL AN APOLOGY. I... I SHOULD NEVER HAVE GOTTEN SO ANGRY AT YOU. AND I SHOULD NEVER HAVE LEFT YOU ALL WITHOUT A MAP TO FIND YOUR WAY. THAT WAS *AWFUL* OF ME.
I THINK WE ALL SAID SOME THINGS THAT WE DIDN'T MEAN. I'M SORRY TOO.
ME TOO. WE SHOULD HAVE TALKED THINGS OUT... LIKE CIVILIZED PONIES. WE ARE IN THIS TOGETHER, AFTER ALL! I'M SORRY.
I'M SORRY EVERYONE. I CAN BE SUCH A HOTHEAD...
RIIIIIGHT... WELL, I'M SORRY... I GUESS.
RAINBOW.
OKAY. OKAY... I'M SORRY TOO.
ME TOO! SORRY EVERYONE!

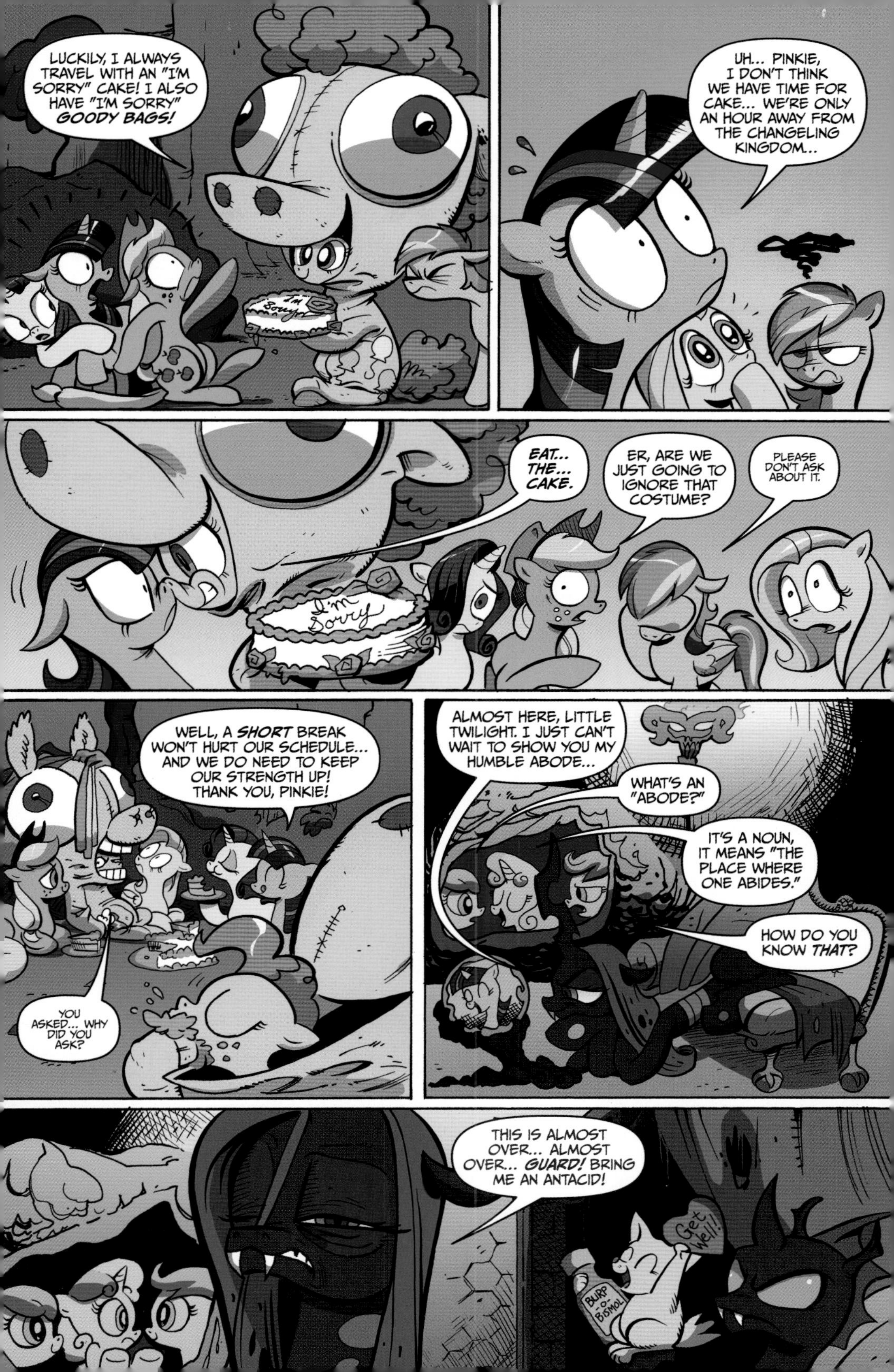
LUCKILY, I ALWAYS TRAVEL WITH AN "I'M SORRY" CAKE! I ALSO HAVE "I'M SORRY" GOODY BAGS!
I'M Sorry
UH... PINKIE, I DON'T THINK WE HAVE TIME FOR CAKE... WE'RE ONLY AN HOUR AWAY FROM THE CHANGELING KINGDOM...
EAT... THE... CAKE.
ER, ARE WE JUST GOING TO IGNORE THAT COSTUME?
PLEASE DON'T ASK ABOUT IT.
I'M Sorry
WELL, A SHORT BREAK WON'T HURT OUR SCHEDULE... AND WE DO NEED TO KEEP OUR STRENGTH UP! THANK YOU, PINKIE!
YOU ASKED... WHY DID YOU ASK?
ALMOST HERE, LITTLE TWILIGHT. I JUST CAN'T WAIT TO SHOW YOU MY HUMBLE ABODE...
WHAT'S AN "ABODE?"
IT'S A NOUN, IT MEANS "THE PLACE WHERE ONE ABIDES."
HOW DO YOU KNOW THAT?
THIS IS ALMOST OVER... ALMOST OVER... GUARD! BRING ME AN ANTACID!
Get Well!
BURP-O-BISMOL

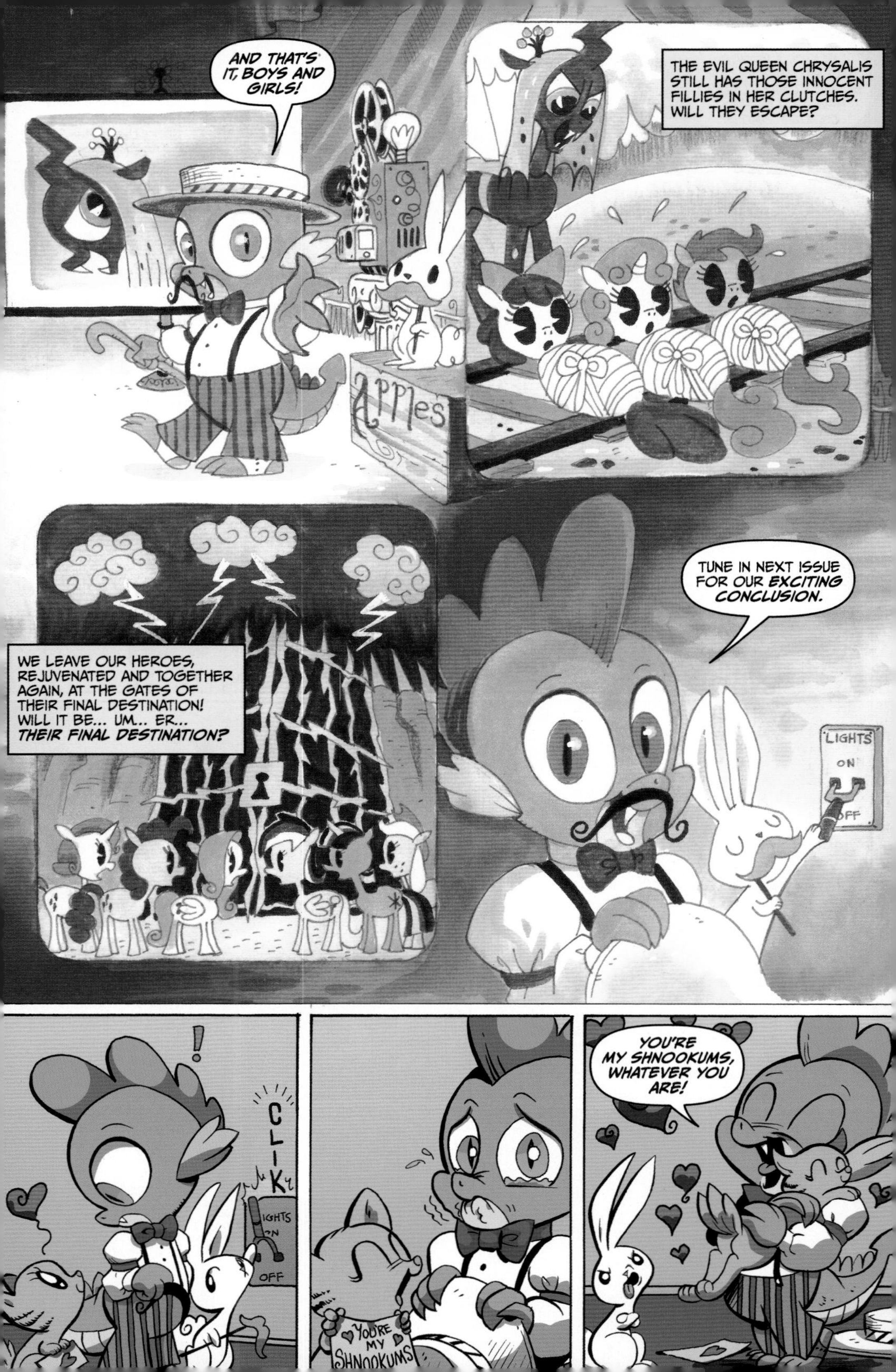
AND THAT'S IT, BOYS AND GIRLS!
THE EVIL QUEEN CHRYSALIS STILL HAS THOSE INNOCENT FILLIES IN HER CLUTCHES. WILL THEY ESCAPE?
APPLES
WE LEAVE OUR HEROES, REJUVENATED AND TOGETHER AGAIN, AT THE GATES OF THEIR FINAL DESTINATION! WILL IT BE... UM... ER... THEIR FINAL DESTINATION?
TUNE IN NEXT ISSUE FOR OUR EXCITING CONCLUSION.
LIGHTS
ON
OFF
!
CLIK
OFF
YOU'RE MY SHNOOKUMS
YOU'RE MY SHNOOKUMS, WHATEVER YOU ARE!

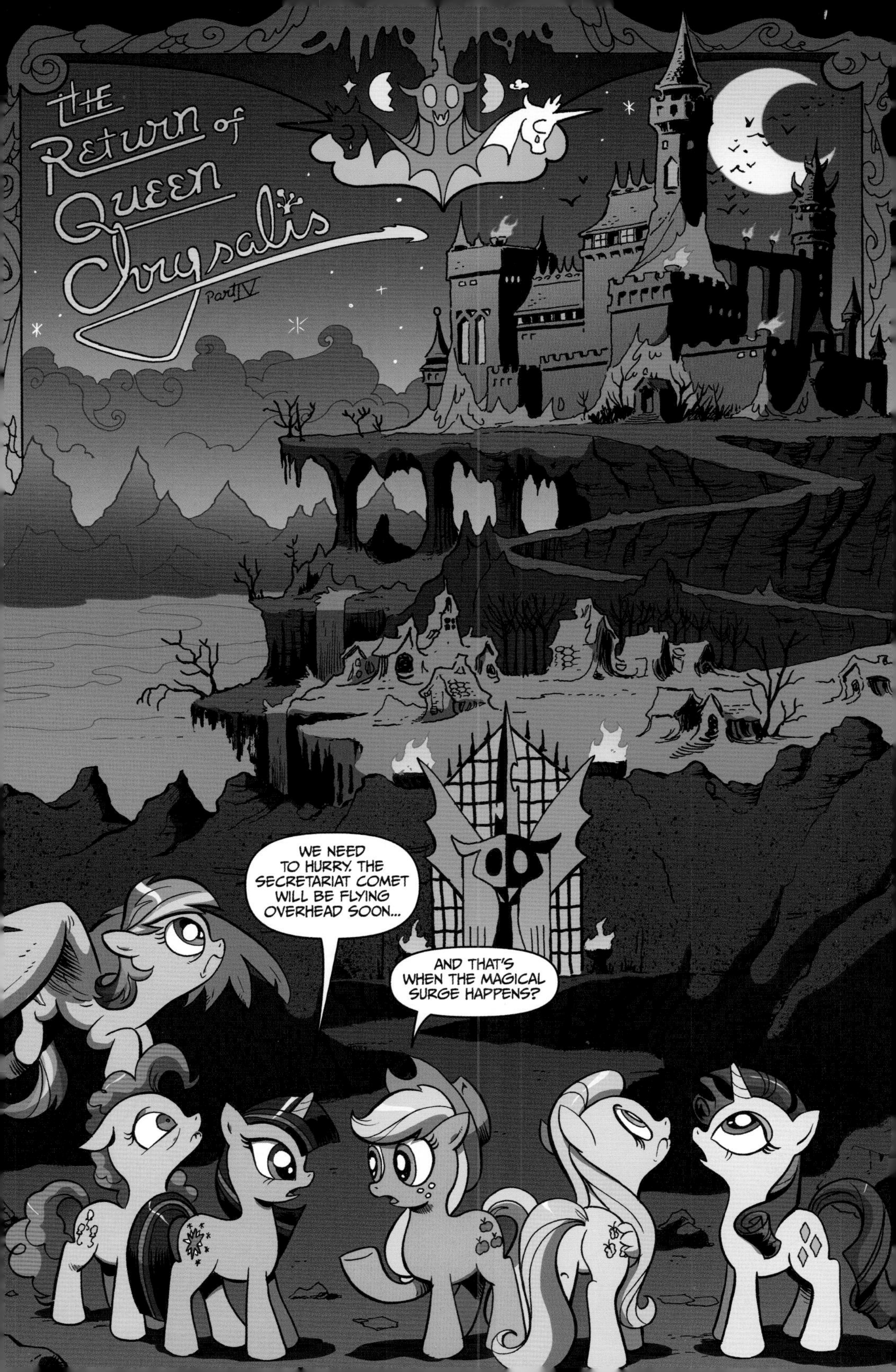
The Return of Queen Chrysalis
Part IV
WE NEED TO HURRY. THE SECRETARIAT COMET WILL BE FLYING OVERHEAD SOON...
AND THAT'S WHEN THE MAGICAL SURGE HAPPENS?

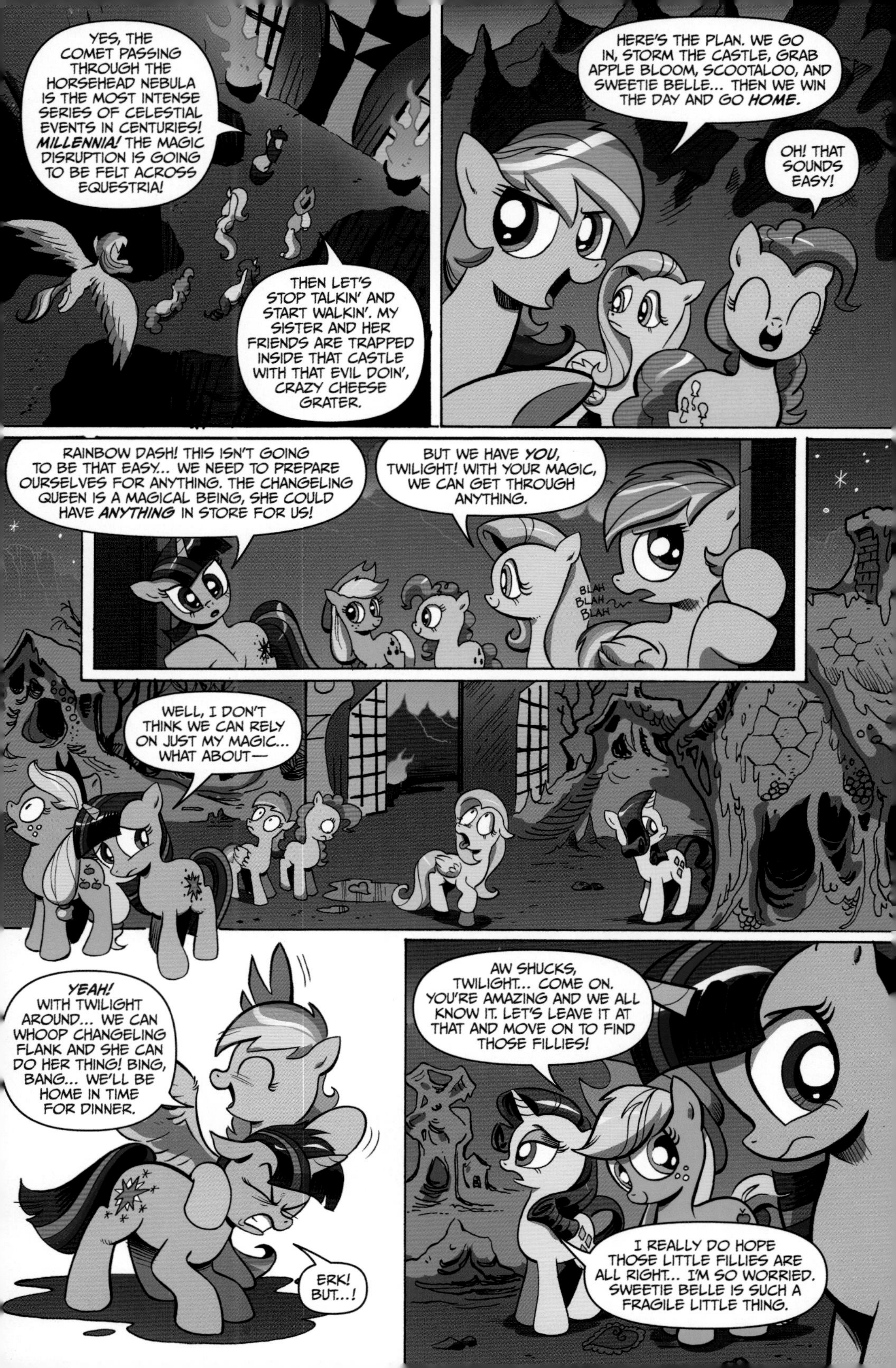
YES, THE COMET PASSING THROUGH THE HORSEHEAD NEBULA IS THE MOST INTENSE SERIES OF CELESTIAL EVENTS IN CENTURIES! *MILLENNIA!* THE MAGIC DISRUPTION IS GOING TO BE FELT ACROSS EQUESTRIA!
THEN LET'S STOP TALKIN' AND START WALKIN'. MY SISTER AND HER FRIENDS ARE TRAPPED INSIDE THAT CASTLE WITH THAT EVIL DOIN', CRAZY CHEESE GRATER.
HERE'S THE PLAN. WE GO IN, STORM THE CASTLE, GRAB APPLE BLOOM, SCOOTALOO, AND SWEETIE BELLE... THEN WE WIN THE DAY AND GO **HOME.**
OH! THAT SOUNDS EASY!
RAINBOW DASH! THIS ISN'T GOING TO BE THAT EASY... WE NEED TO PREPARE OURSELVES FOR ANYTHING. THE CHANGELING QUEEN IS A MAGICAL BEING, SHE COULD HAVE *ANYTHING* IN STORE FOR US!
BUT WE HAVE *YOU*, TWILIGHT! WITH YOUR MAGIC, WE CAN GET THROUGH ANYTHING.
BLAH BLAH BLAH
WELL, I DON'T THINK WE CAN RELY ON JUST MY MAGIC... WHAT ABOUT—
YEAH! WITH TWILIGHT AROUND... WE CAN WHOOP CHANGELING FLANK AND SHE CAN DO HER THING! BING, BANG... WE'LL BE HOME IN TIME FOR DINNER.
ERK! BUT...!
AW SHUCKS, TWILIGHT... COME ON. YOU'RE AMAZING AND WE ALL KNOW IT. LET'S LEAVE IT AT THAT AND MOVE ON TO FIND THOSE FILLIES!
I REALLY DO HOPE THOSE LITTLE FILLIES ARE ALL RIGHT... I'M SO WORRIED. SWEETIE BELLE IS SUCH A FRAGILE LITTLE THING.

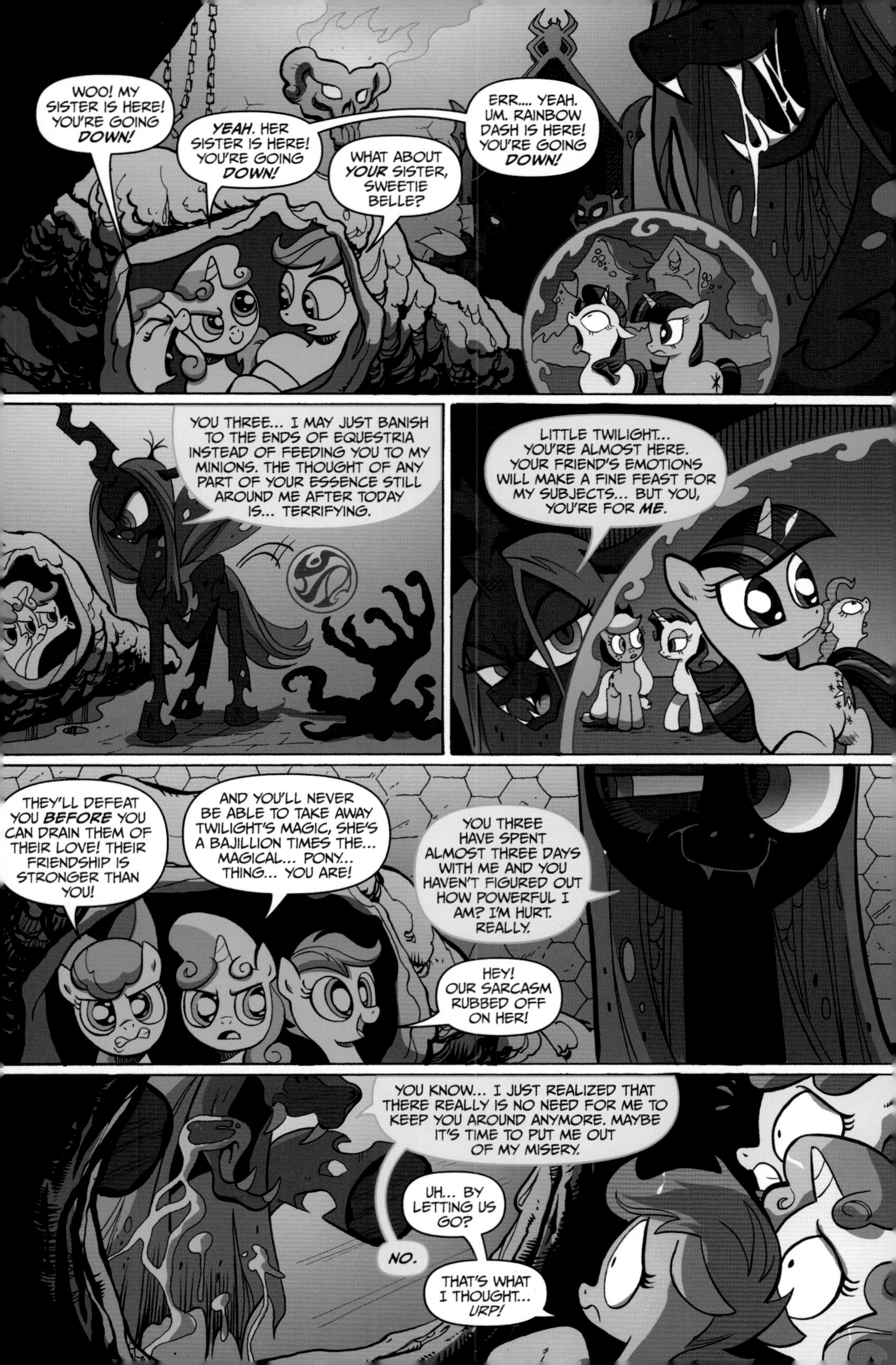
WOO! MY SISTER IS HERE! YOU'RE GOING DOWN!
YEAH. HER SISTER IS HERE! YOU'RE GOING DOWN!
WHAT ABOUT YOUR SISTER, SWEETIE BELLE?
ERR.... YEAH. UM. RAINBOW DASH IS HERE! YOU'RE GOING DOWN!
YOU THREE... I MAY JUST BANISH TO THE ENDS OF EQUESTRIA INSTEAD OF FEEDING YOU TO MY MINIONS. THE THOUGHT OF ANY PART OF YOUR ESSENCE STILL AROUND ME AFTER TODAY IS... TERRIFYING.
LITTLE TWILIGHT... YOU'RE ALMOST HERE. YOUR FRIEND'S EMOTIONS WILL MAKE A FINE FEAST FOR MY SUBJECTS... BUT YOU, YOU'RE FOR ME.
THEY'LL DEFEAT YOU BEFORE YOU CAN DRAIN THEM OF THEIR LOVE! THEIR FRIENDSHIP IS STRONGER THAN YOU!
AND YOU'LL NEVER BE ABLE TO TAKE AWAY TWILIGHT'S MAGIC, SHE'S A BAJILLION TIMES THE... MAGICAL... PONY... THING... YOU ARE!
YOU THREE HAVE SPENT ALMOST THREE DAYS WITH ME AND YOU HAVEN'T FIGURED OUT HOW POWERFUL I AM? I'M HURT. REALLY.
HEY! OUR SARCASM RUBBED OFF ON HER!
YOU KNOW... I JUST REALIZED THAT THERE REALLY IS NO NEED FOR ME TO KEEP YOU AROUND ANYMORE. MAYBE IT'S TIME TO PUT ME OUT OF MY MISERY.
UH... BY LETTING US GO?
NO.
THAT'S WHAT I THOUGHT... URP!

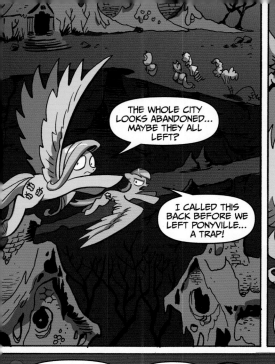

THE WHOLE CITY LOOKS ABANDONED... MAYBE THEY ALL LEFT?

I CALLED THIS BACK BEFORE WE LEFT PONYVILLE... A TRAP!

DOESN'T SHE HAVE A WHOLE ARMY? WHERE IS EVERYPONY?

THEY HAVE TO BE INSIDE THE CASTLE... THERE'S JUST NO WAY SHE WOULD BRING US HERE AND BE GONE!

OH! OH! I BET THEY'RE ALL WAITING FOR US RIGHT BEHIND THE FRONT DOOR! *THOUSANDS* OF CHANGELINGS, READY AND WAITING... POISED TO *STRIKE!*

GEE... I WONDER WHY THAT MAKES ME WANT TO OPEN THE DOOR *LESS.*

THOUSANDS?

NO WORRIES... I STILL HAVE *THIS!*

TA DA!

PINKIE... *NO.* I TOLD YOU BACK IN THE VALLEY... *NO.* TAKE THAT *OFF.*

BUT I BROUGHT IT ALL THE WAY FROM PONYVILLE! I KNOW IT'LL HELP! JUST YOU WAIT!

THIS IS NO TIME TO BE HORSIN' AROUND! WE'VE GOT TO GET INTO THAT CASTLE AND...

FOOP

CREEEAK

CREEEEAAKKK

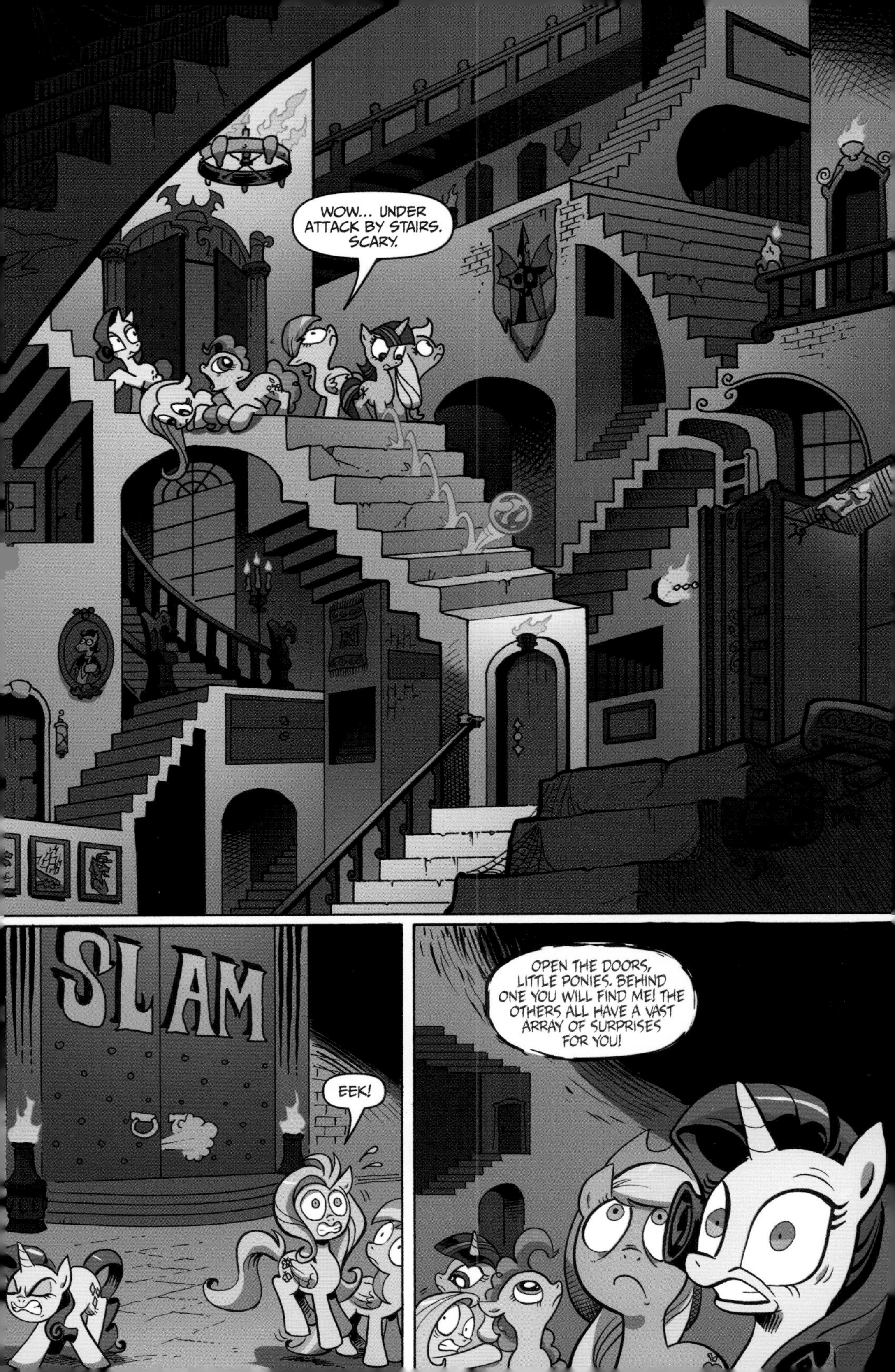

WOW... UNDER ATTACK BY STAIRS. SCARY.
SLAM
EEK!
OPEN THE DOORS, LITTLE PONIES. BEHIND ONE YOU WILL FIND ME! THE OTHERS ALL HAVE A VAST ARRAY OF SURPRISES FOR YOU!

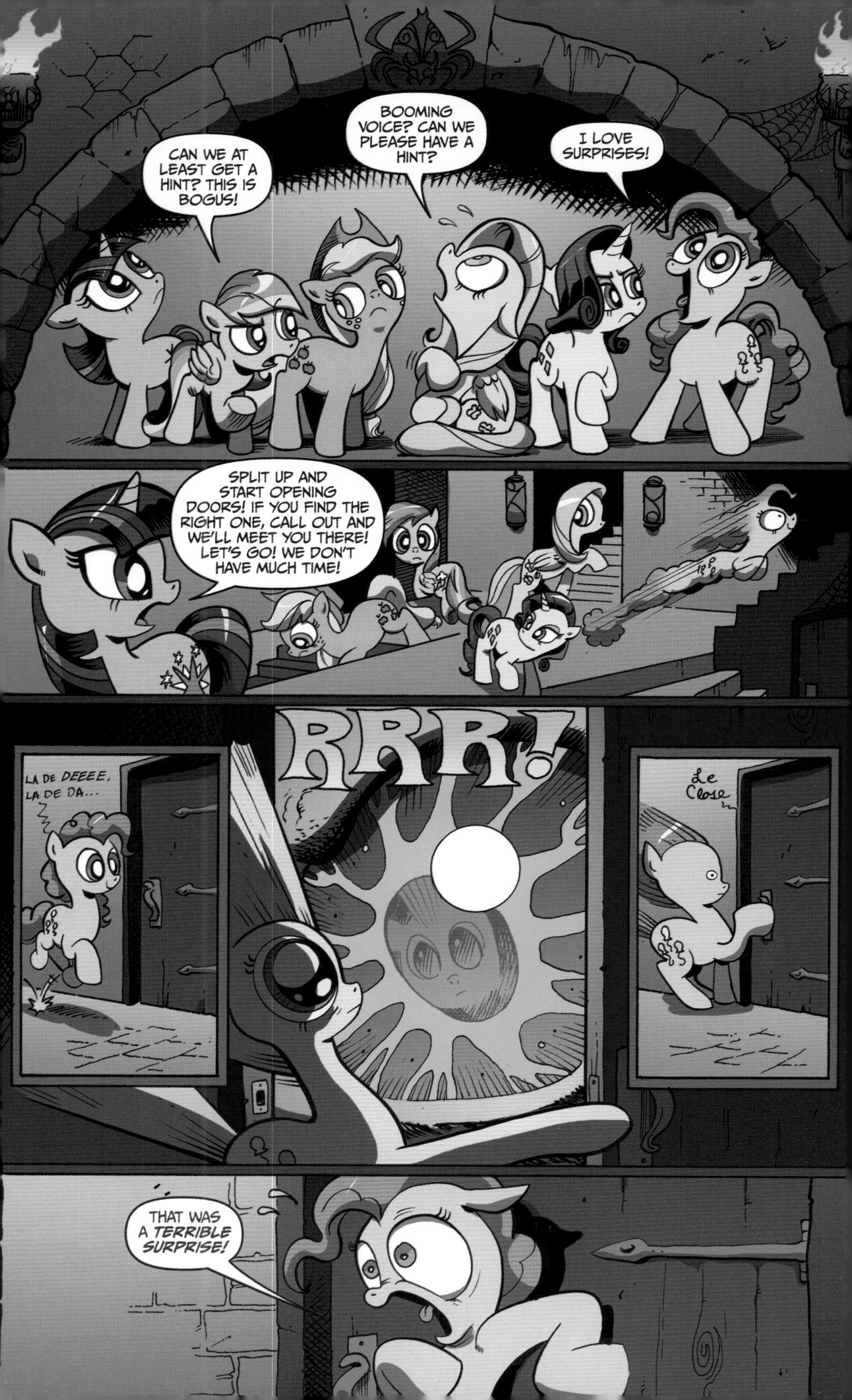
CAN WE AT LEAST GET A HINT? THIS IS BOGUS!
BOOMING VOICE? CAN WE PLEASE HAVE A HINT?
I LOVE SURPRISES!
SPLIT UP AND START OPENING DOORS! IF YOU FIND THE RIGHT ONE, CALL OUT AND WE'LL MEET YOU THERE! LET'S GO! WE DON'T HAVE MUCH TIME!
LA DE DEEEE, LA DE DA...
RRR!
Le Close
THAT WAS A *TERRIBLE SURPRISE!*

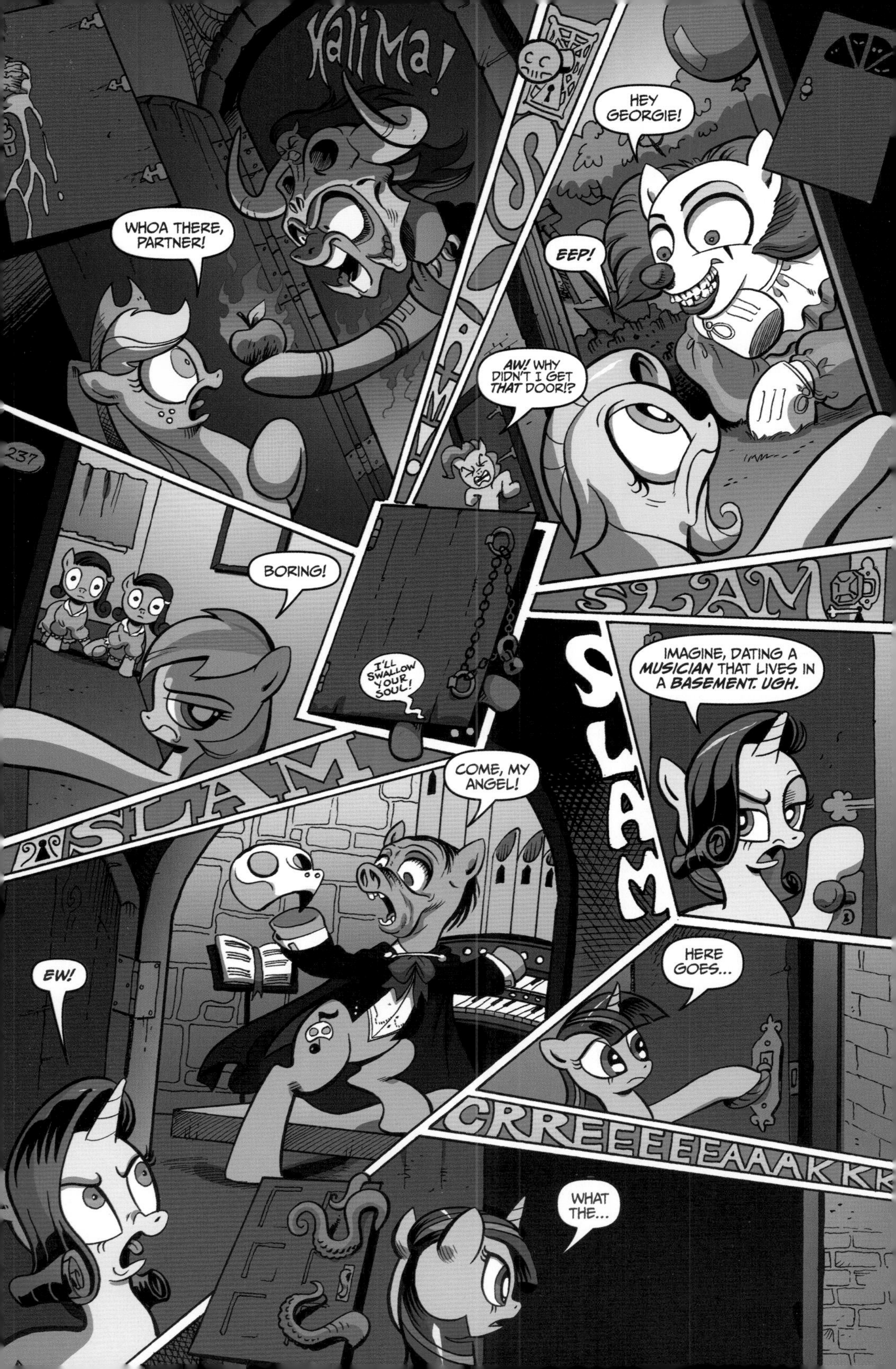
KALIMA!
WHOA THERE, PARTNER!
HEY GEORGIE!
EEP!
AW! WHY DIDN'T I GET THAT DOOR!?
237
BORING!
I'LL SWALLOW YOUR SOUL!
SLAM
SLAM
IMAGINE, DATING A MUSICIAN THAT LIVES IN A BASEMENT. UGH.
SLAM
COME, MY ANGEL!
EW!
HERE GOES...
CRREEEEEEAAAKK
WHAT THE...

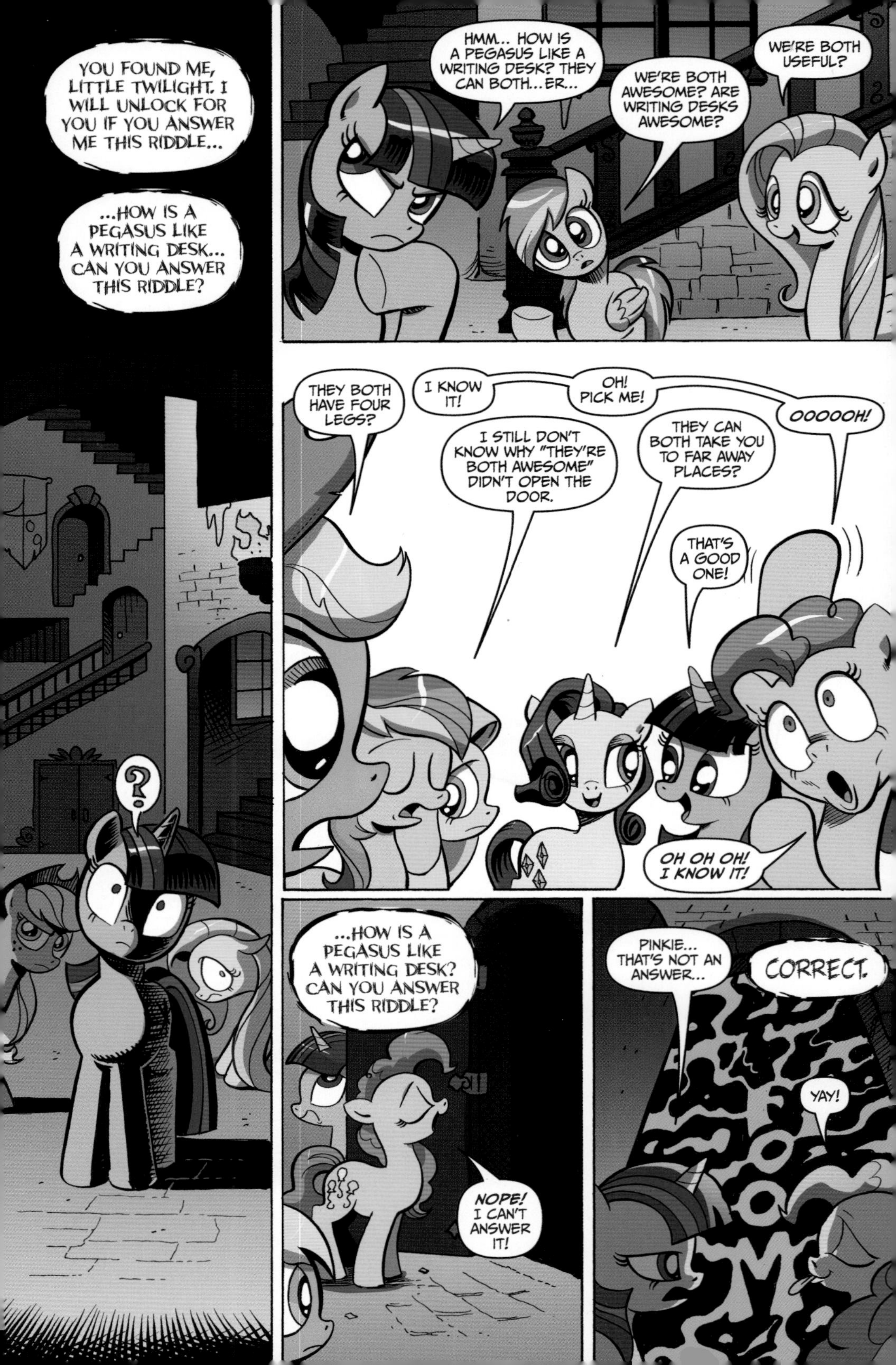
YOU FOUND ME, LITTLE TWILIGHT. I WILL UNLOCK FOR YOU IF YOU ANSWER ME THIS RIDDLE...
...HOW IS A PEGASUS LIKE A WRITING DESK... CAN YOU ANSWER THIS RIDDLE?
?
HMM... HOW IS A PEGASUS LIKE A WRITING DESK? THEY CAN BOTH...ER...
WE'RE BOTH AWESOME? ARE WRITING DESKS AWESOME?
WE'RE BOTH USEFUL?
THEY BOTH HAVE FOUR LEGS?
I KNOW IT!
OH! PICK ME!
OOOOOH!
I STILL DON'T KNOW WHY "THEY'RE BOTH AWESOME" DIDN'T OPEN THE DOOR.
THEY CAN BOTH TAKE YOU TO FAR AWAY PLACES?
THAT'S A GOOD ONE!
OH OH OH! I KNOW IT!
...HOW IS A PEGASUS LIKE A WRITING DESK? CAN YOU ANSWER THIS RIDDLE?
NOPE! I CAN'T ANSWER IT!
PINKIE... THAT'S NOT AN ANSWER...
CORRECT.
YAY!

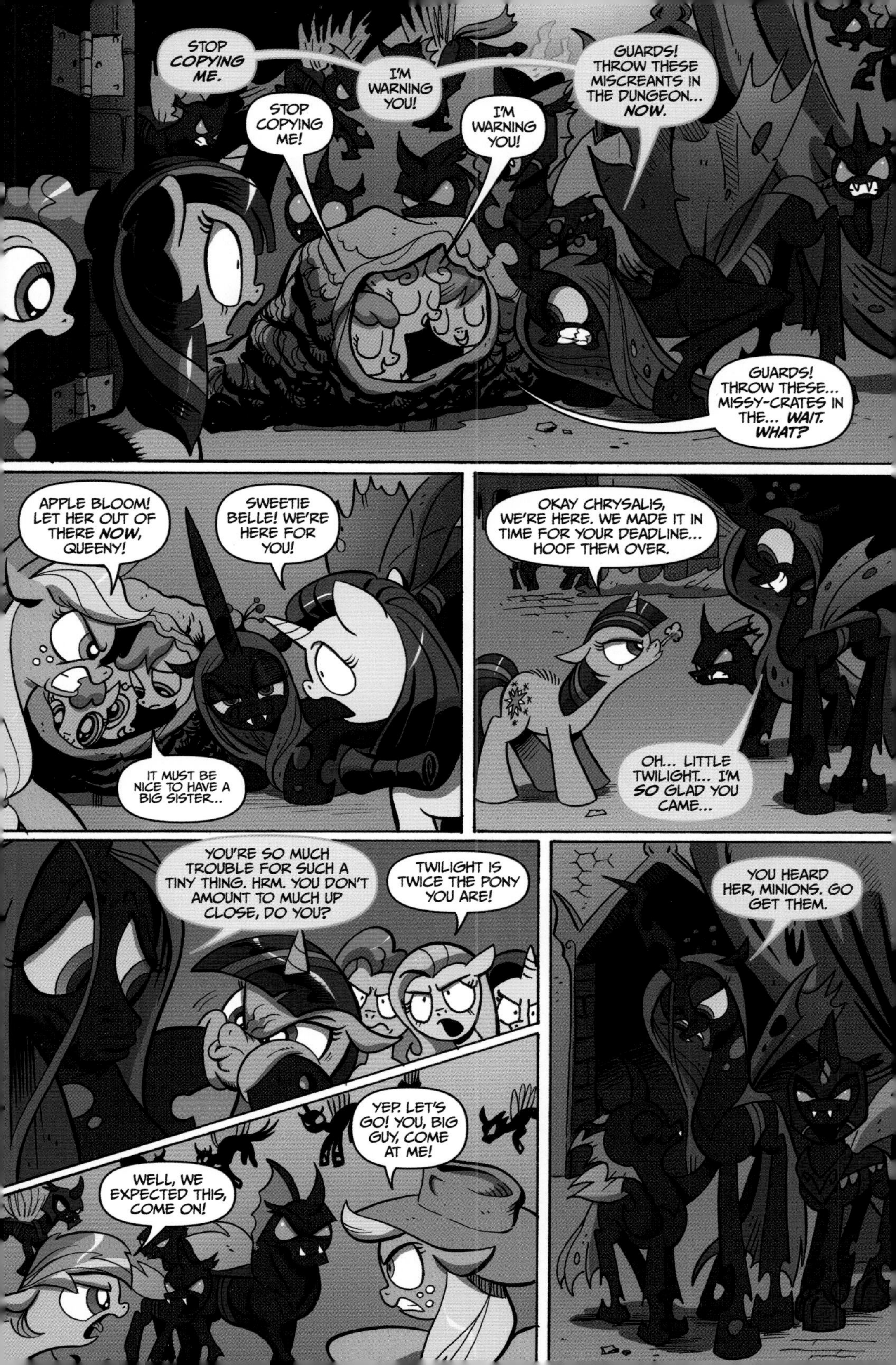
STOP COPYING ME.
I'M WARNING YOU!
GUARDS! THROW THESE MISCREANTS IN THE DUNGEON... NOW.
STOP COPYING ME!
I'M WARNING YOU!
GUARDS! THROW THESE... MISSY-CRATES IN THE... WAIT. WHAT?
APPLE BLOOM! LET HER OUT OF THERE NOW, QUEENY!
SWEETIE BELLE! WE'RE HERE FOR YOU!
IT MUST BE NICE TO HAVE A BIG SISTER...
OKAY CHRYSALIS, WE'RE HERE. WE MADE IT IN TIME FOR YOUR DEADLINE... HOOF THEM OVER.
OH... LITTLE TWILIGHT... I'M SO GLAD YOU CAME...
YOU'RE SO MUCH TROUBLE FOR SUCH A TINY THING. HRM. YOU DON'T AMOUNT TO MUCH UP CLOSE, DO YOU?
TWILIGHT IS TWICE THE PONY YOU ARE!
YOU HEARD HER, MINIONS. GO GET THEM.
YEP. LET'S GO! YOU, BIG GUY, COME AT ME!
WELL, WE EXPECTED THIS, COME ON!

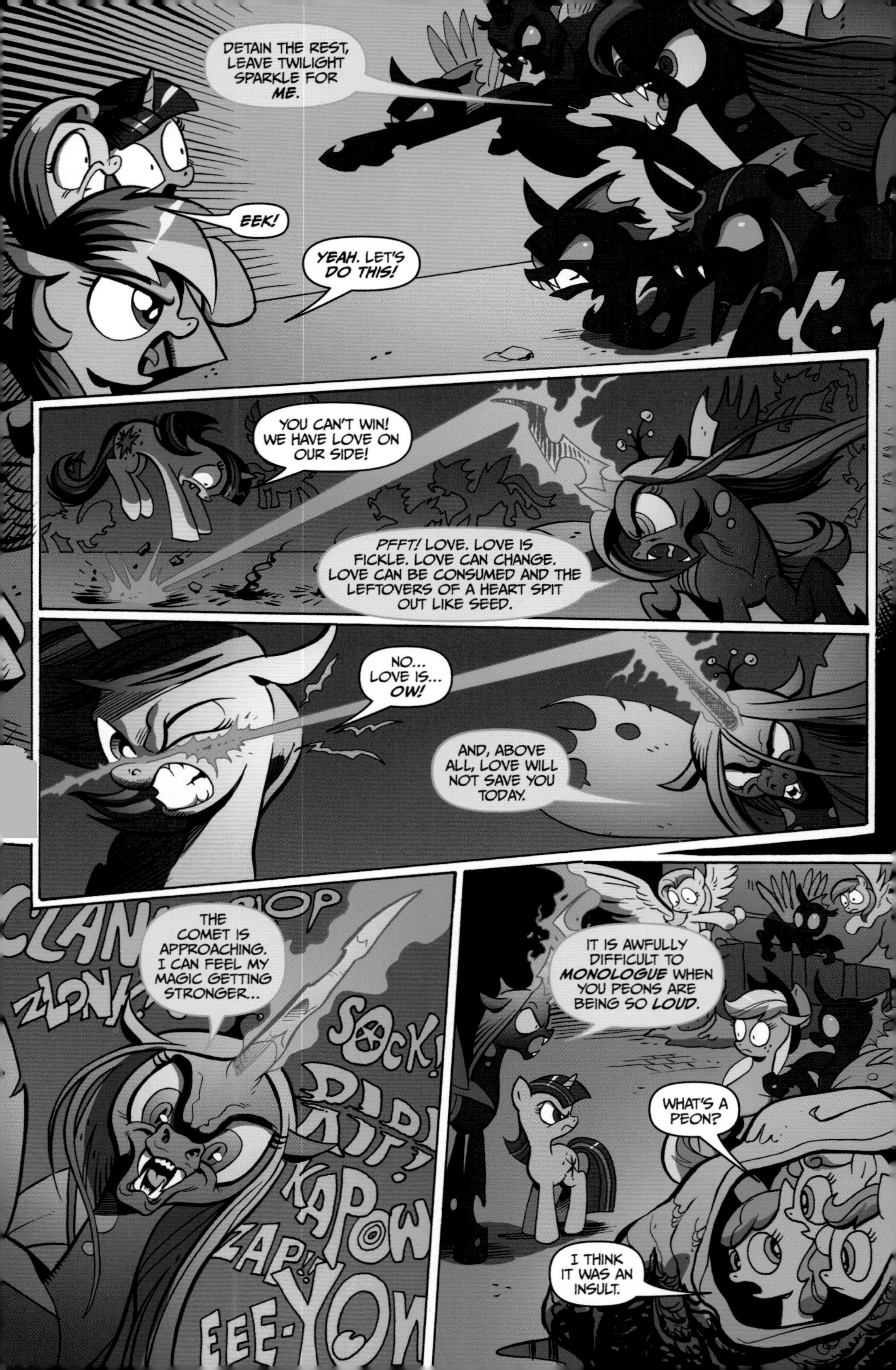
DETAIN THE REST, LEAVE TWILIGHT SPARKLE FOR ME.
EEK!
YEAH. LET'S DO THIS!
YOU CAN'T WIN! WE HAVE LOVE ON OUR SIDE!
PFFT! LOVE. LOVE IS FICKLE. LOVE CAN CHANGE. LOVE CAN BE CONSUMED AND THE LEFTOVERS OF A HEART SPIT OUT LIKE SEED.
NO... LOVE IS... OW!
AND, ABOVE ALL, LOVE WILL NOT SAVE YOU TODAY.
THE COMET IS APPROACHING. I CAN FEEL MY MAGIC GETTING STRONGER...
SOCK!
KAPOW
ZAP!!
FEE-YOW
IT IS AWFULLY DIFFICULT TO MONOLOGUE WHEN YOU PEONS ARE BEING SO LOUD.
WHAT'S A PEON?
I THINK IT WAS AN INSULT.

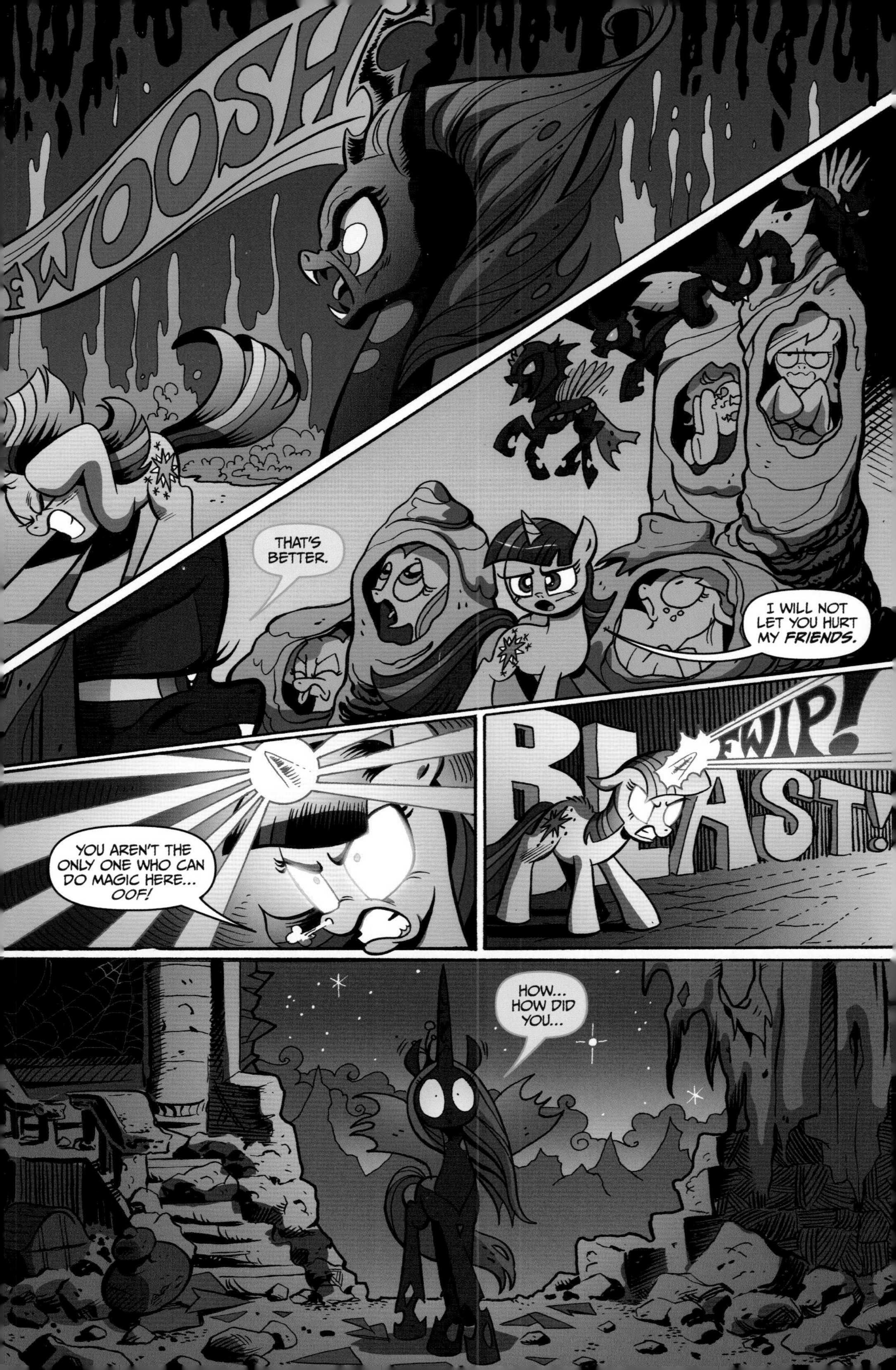
FWOOSH
THAT'S BETTER.
I WILL NOT LET YOU HURT MY FRIENDS.
YOU AREN'T THE ONLY ONE WHO CAN DO MAGIC HERE... OOF!
FWIP!
BLAST!
HOW... HOW DID YOU...

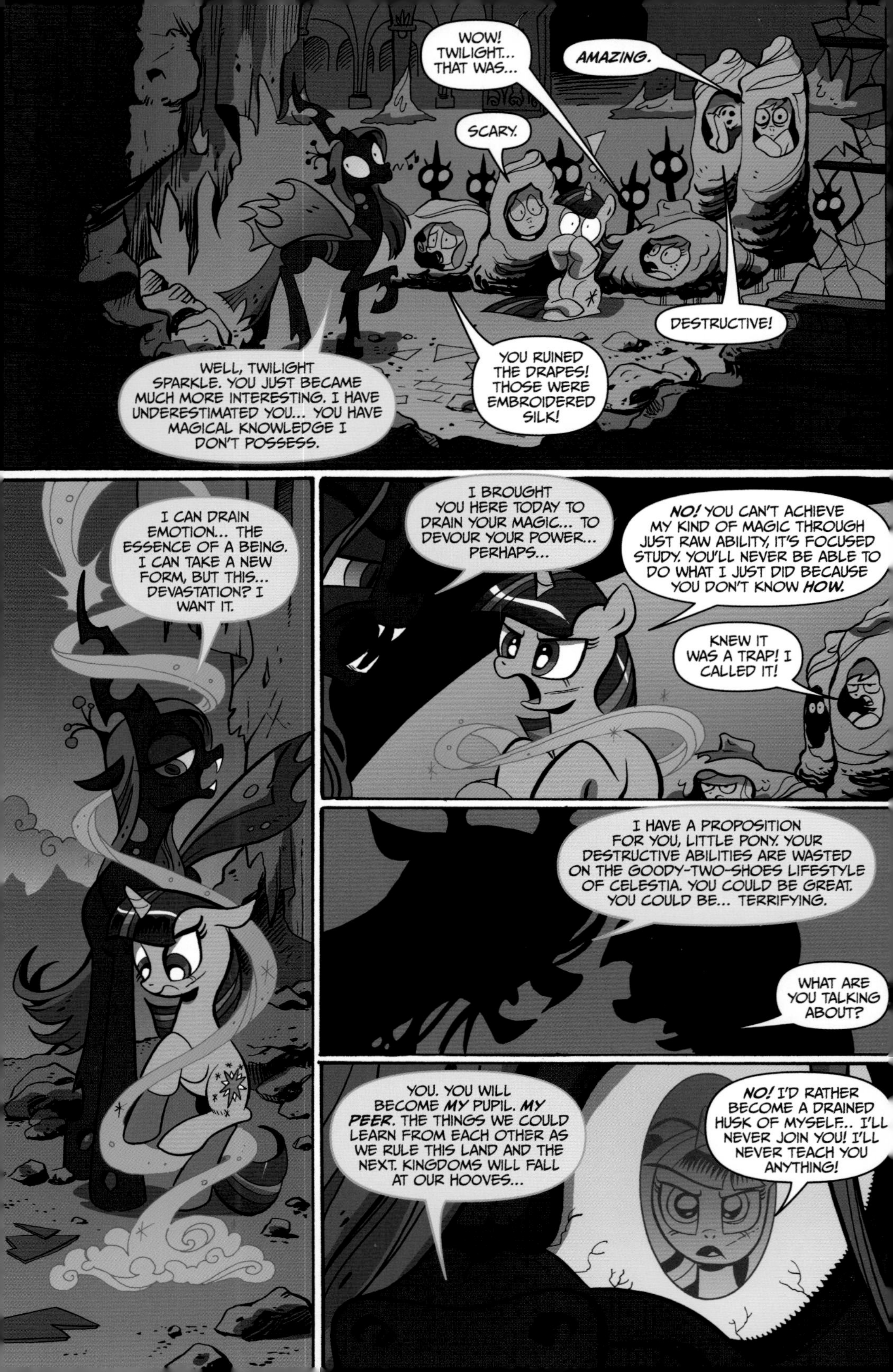
WOW! TWILIGHT... THAT WAS...
AMAZING.
SCARY.
DESTRUCTIVE!
YOU RUINED THE DRAPES! THOSE WERE EMBROIDERED SILK!
WELL, TWILIGHT SPARKLE. YOU JUST BECAME MUCH MORE INTERESTING. I HAVE UNDERESTIMATED YOU... YOU HAVE MAGICAL KNOWLEDGE I DON'T POSSESS.
I CAN DRAIN EMOTION... THE ESSENCE OF A BEING. I CAN TAKE A NEW FORM, BUT THIS... DEVASTATION? I WANT IT.
I BROUGHT YOU HERE TODAY TO DRAIN YOUR MAGIC... TO DEVOUR YOUR POWER... PERHAPS...
NO! YOU CAN'T ACHIEVE MY KIND OF MAGIC THROUGH JUST RAW ABILITY, IT'S FOCUSED STUDY. YOU'LL NEVER BE ABLE TO DO WHAT I JUST DID BECAUSE YOU DON'T KNOW HOW.
KNEW IT WAS A TRAP! I CALLED IT!
I HAVE A PROPOSITION FOR YOU, LITTLE PONY. YOUR DESTRUCTIVE ABILITIES ARE WASTED ON THE GOODY-TWO-SHOES LIFESTYLE OF CELESTIA. YOU COULD BE GREAT. YOU COULD BE... TERRIFYING.
WHAT ARE YOU TALKING ABOUT?
YOU. YOU WILL BECOME MY PUPIL. MY PEER. THE THINGS WE COULD LEARN FROM EACH OTHER AS WE RULE THIS LAND AND THE NEXT. KINGDOMS WILL FALL AT OUR HOOVES...
NO! I'D RATHER BECOME A DRAINED HUSK OF MYSELF... I'LL NEVER JOIN YOU! I'LL NEVER TEACH YOU ANYTHING!

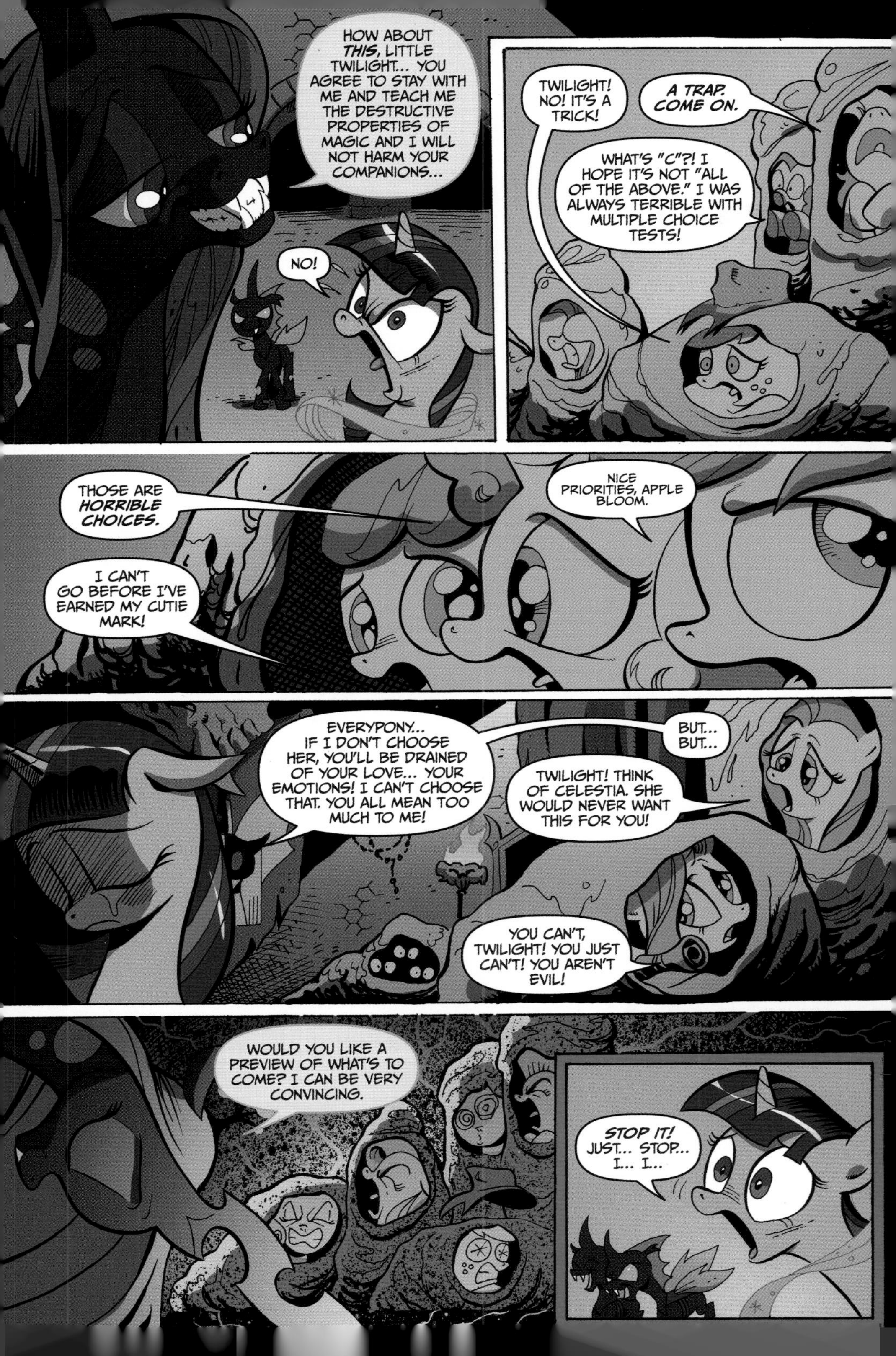
HOW ABOUT *THIS*, LITTLE TWILIGHT... YOU AGREE TO STAY WITH ME AND TEACH ME THE DESTRUCTIVE PROPERTIES OF MAGIC AND I WILL NOT HARM YOUR COMPANIONS...
NO!
TWILIGHT! NO! IT'S A TRICK!
A TRAP. COME ON.
WHAT'S "C"?! I HOPE IT'S NOT "ALL OF THE ABOVE." I WAS ALWAYS TERRIBLE WITH MULTIPLE CHOICE TESTS!
THOSE ARE *HORRIBLE CHOICES.*
NICE PRIORITIES, APPLE BLOOM.
I CAN'T GO BEFORE I'VE EARNED MY CUTIE MARK!
EVERYPONY... IF I DON'T CHOOSE HER, YOU'LL BE DRAINED OF YOUR LOVE... YOUR EMOTIONS! I CAN'T CHOOSE THAT. YOU ALL MEAN TOO MUCH TO ME!
BUT... BUT...
TWILIGHT! THINK OF CELESTIA. SHE WOULD NEVER WANT THIS FOR YOU!
YOU CAN'T, TWILIGHT! YOU JUST CAN'T! YOU AREN'T EVIL!
WOULD YOU LIKE A PREVIEW OF WHAT'S TO COME? I CAN BE VERY CONVINCING.
STOP IT! JUST... STOP... I... I...

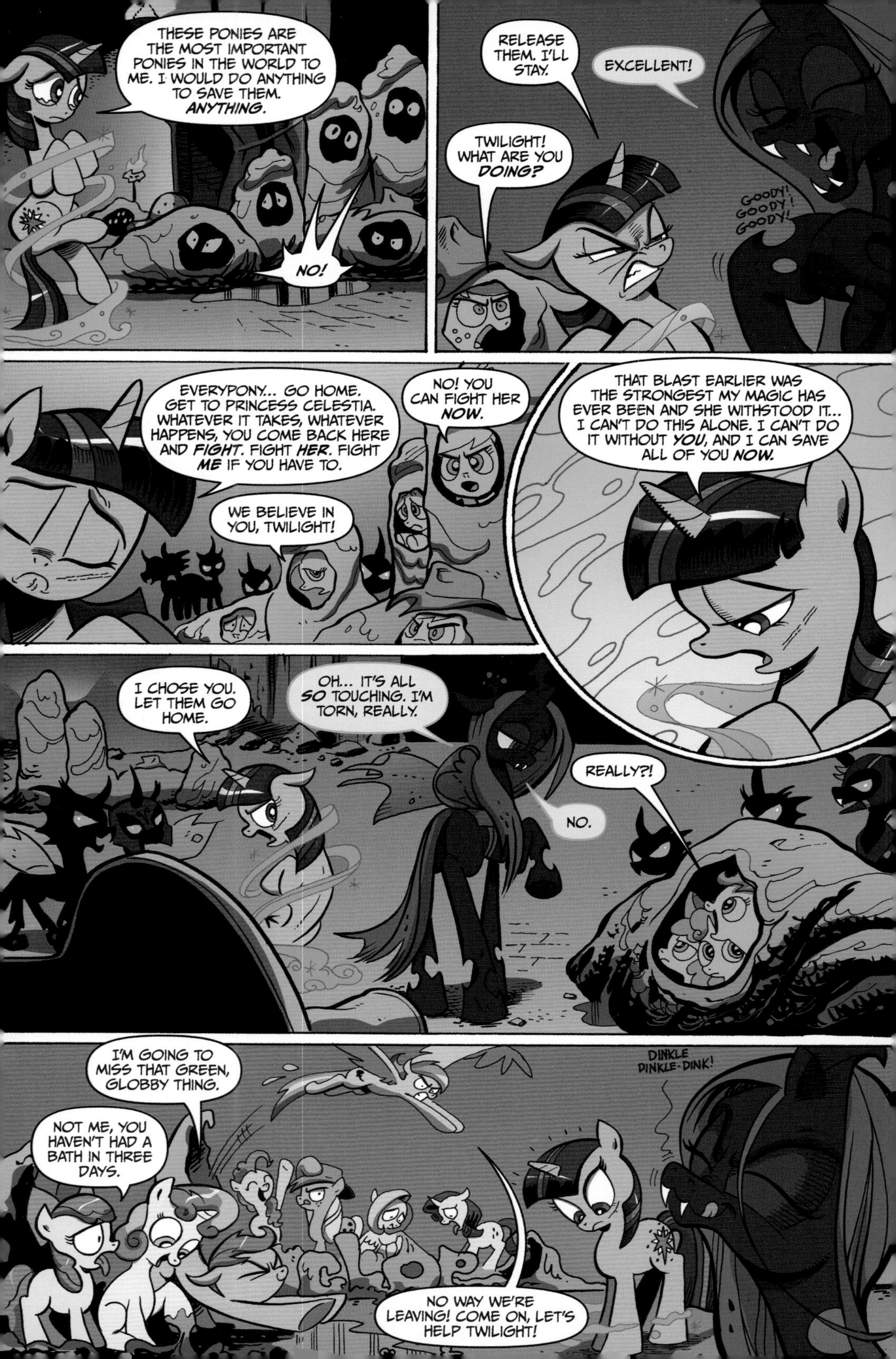
THESE PONIES ARE THE MOST IMPORTANT PONIES IN THE WORLD TO ME. I WOULD DO ANYTHING TO SAVE THEM. ANYTHING.
NO!
RELEASE THEM. I'LL STAY.
EXCELLENT!
TWILIGHT! WHAT ARE YOU DOING?
GOODY! GOODY! GOODY!
EVERYPONY... GO HOME. GET TO PRINCESS CELESTIA. WHATEVER IT TAKES, WHATEVER HAPPENS, YOU COME BACK HERE AND FIGHT. FIGHT HER. FIGHT ME IF YOU HAVE TO.
NO! YOU CAN FIGHT HER NOW.
WE BELIEVE IN YOU, TWILIGHT!
THAT BLAST EARLIER WAS THE STRONGEST MY MAGIC HAS EVER BEEN AND SHE WITHSTOOD IT... I CAN'T DO THIS ALONE. I CAN'T DO IT WITHOUT YOU, AND I CAN SAVE ALL OF YOU NOW.
I CHOSE YOU. LET THEM GO HOME.
OH... IT'S ALL SO TOUCHING. I'M TORN, REALLY.
REALLY?!
NO.
I'M GOING TO MISS THAT GREEN, GLOBBY THING.
NOT ME, YOU HAVEN'T HAD A BATH IN THREE DAYS.
DINKLE DINKLE-DINK!
NO WAY WE'RE LEAVING! COME ON, LET'S HELP TWILIGHT!

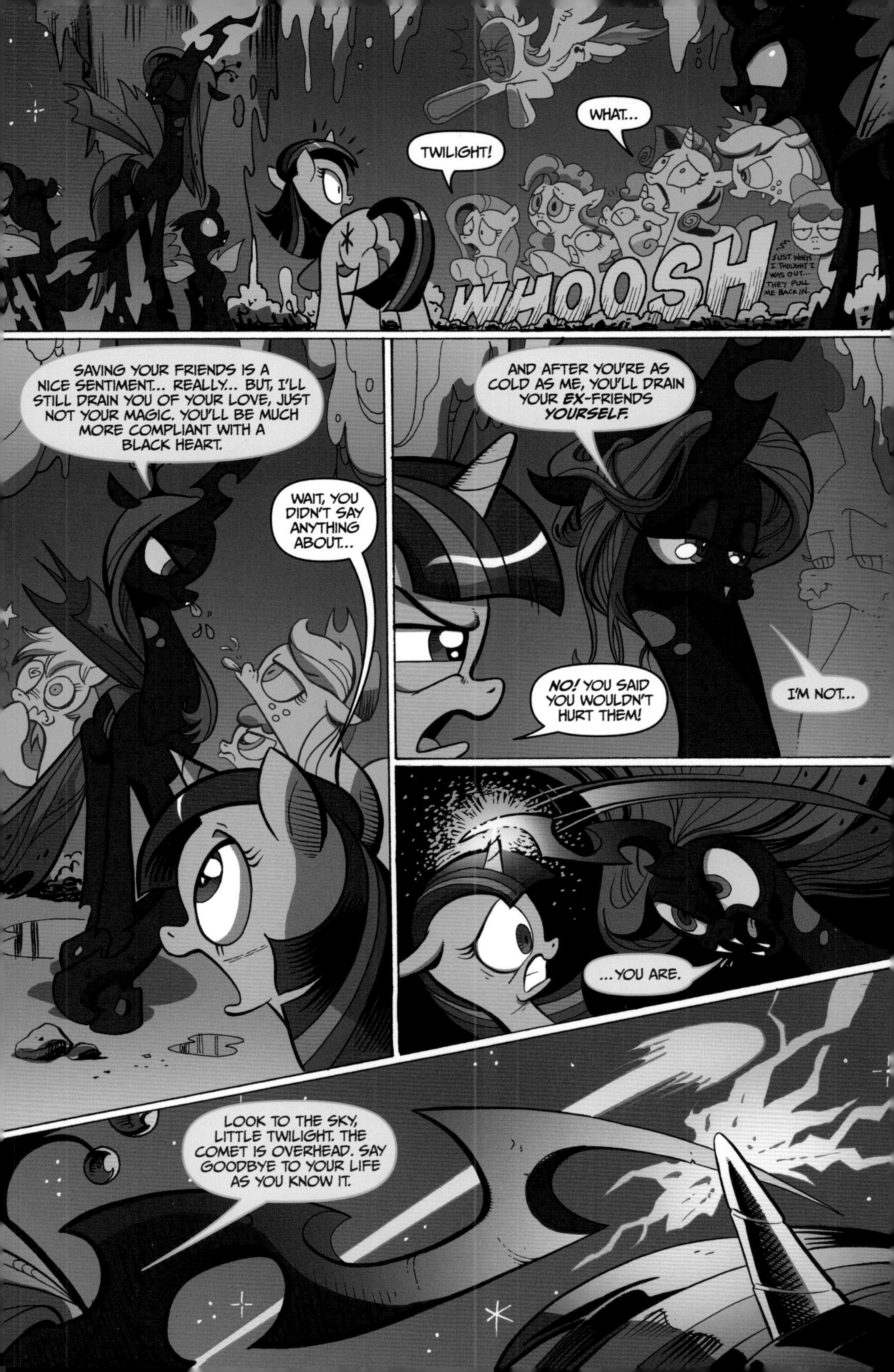
TWILIGHT!
WHAT...
WHOOSH
JUST WHEN I THOUGHT I WAS OUT... THEY PULL ME BACK IN.
SAVING YOUR FRIENDS IS A NICE SENTIMENT... REALLY... BUT, I'LL STILL DRAIN YOU OF YOUR LOVE, JUST NOT YOUR MAGIC. YOU'LL BE MUCH MORE COMPLIANT WITH A BLACK HEART.
WAIT, YOU DIDN'T SAY ANYTHING ABOUT...
AND AFTER YOU'RE AS COLD AS ME, YOU'LL DRAIN YOUR EX-FRIENDS YOURSELF.
NO! YOU SAID YOU WOULDN'T HURT THEM!
I'M NOT...
...YOU ARE.
LOOK TO THE SKY, LITTLE TWILIGHT. THE COMET IS OVERHEAD. SAY GOODBYE TO YOUR LIFE AS YOU KNOW IT.

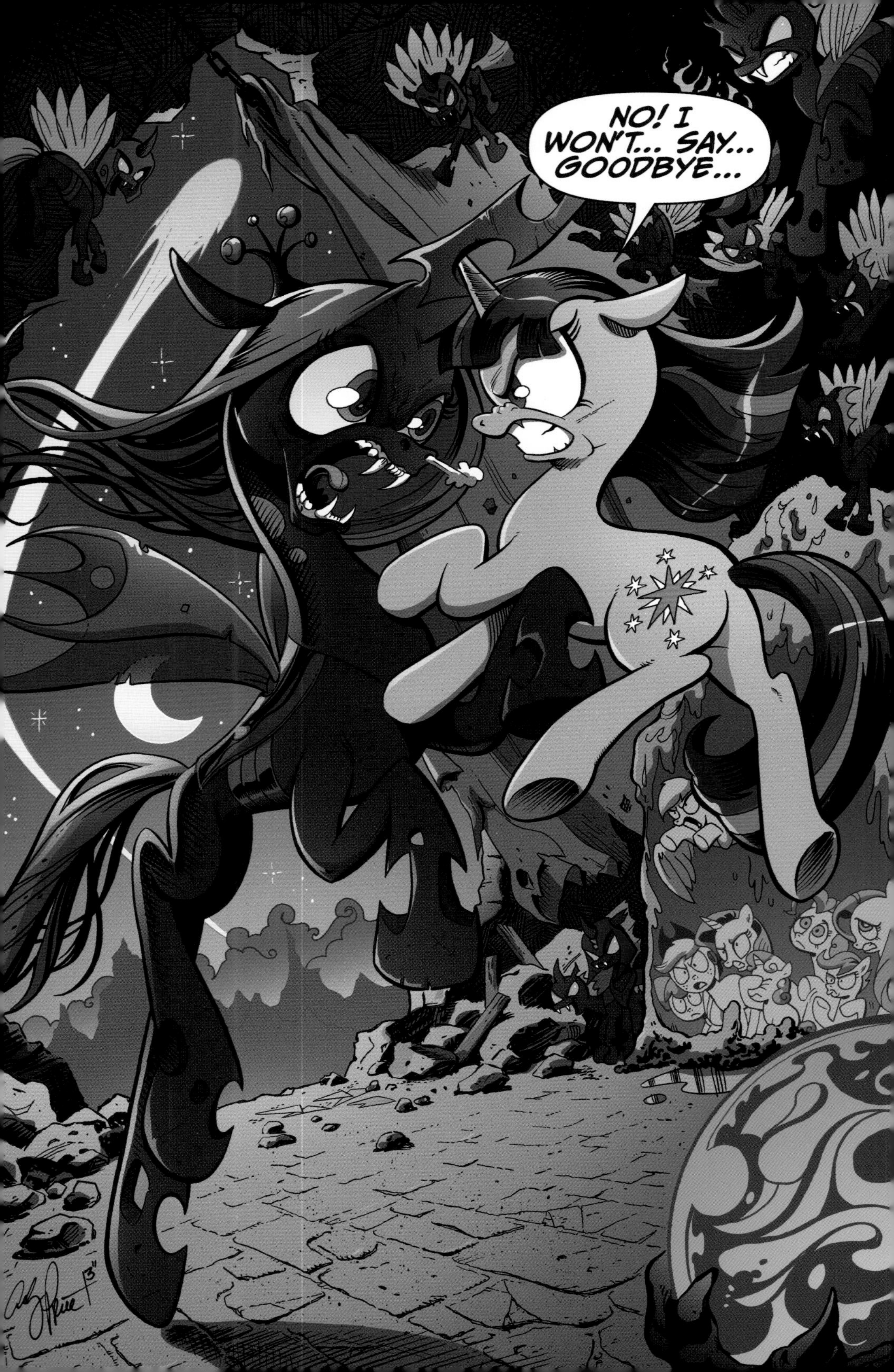
NO! I WON'T... SAY... GOODBYE...

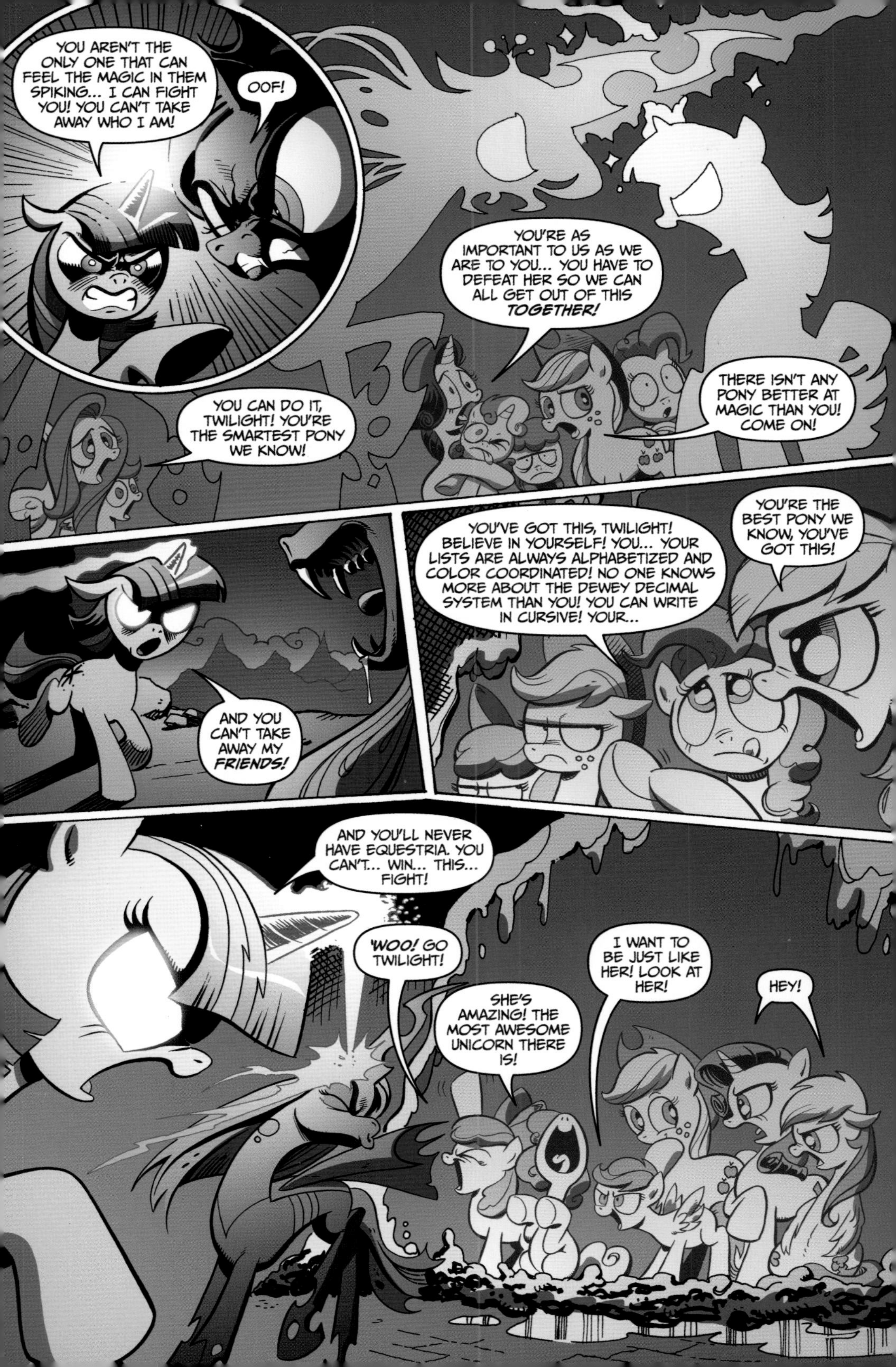
YOU AREN'T THE ONLY ONE THAT CAN FEEL THE MAGIC IN THEM SPIKING... I CAN FIGHT YOU! YOU CAN'T TAKE AWAY WHO I AM!
OOF!
YOU'RE AS IMPORTANT TO US AS WE ARE TO YOU... YOU HAVE TO DEFEAT HER SO WE CAN ALL GET OUT OF THIS TOGETHER!
YOU CAN DO IT, TWILIGHT! YOU'RE THE SMARTEST PONY WE KNOW!
THERE ISN'T ANY PONY BETTER AT MAGIC THAN YOU! COME ON!
AND YOU CAN'T TAKE AWAY MY FRIENDS!
YOU'VE GOT THIS, TWILIGHT! BELIEVE IN YOURSELF! YOU... YOUR LISTS ARE ALWAYS ALPHABETIZED AND COLOR COORDINATED! NO ONE KNOWS MORE ABOUT THE DEWEY DECIMAL SYSTEM THAN YOU! YOU CAN WRITE IN CURSIVE! YOUR...
YOU'RE THE BEST PONY WE KNOW, YOU'VE GOT THIS!
AND YOU'LL NEVER HAVE EQUESTRIA. YOU CAN'T... WIN... THIS... FIGHT!
'WOO! GO TWILIGHT!
SHE'S AMAZING! THE MOST AWESOME UNICORN THERE IS!
I WANT TO BE JUST LIKE HER! LOOK AT HER!
HEY!

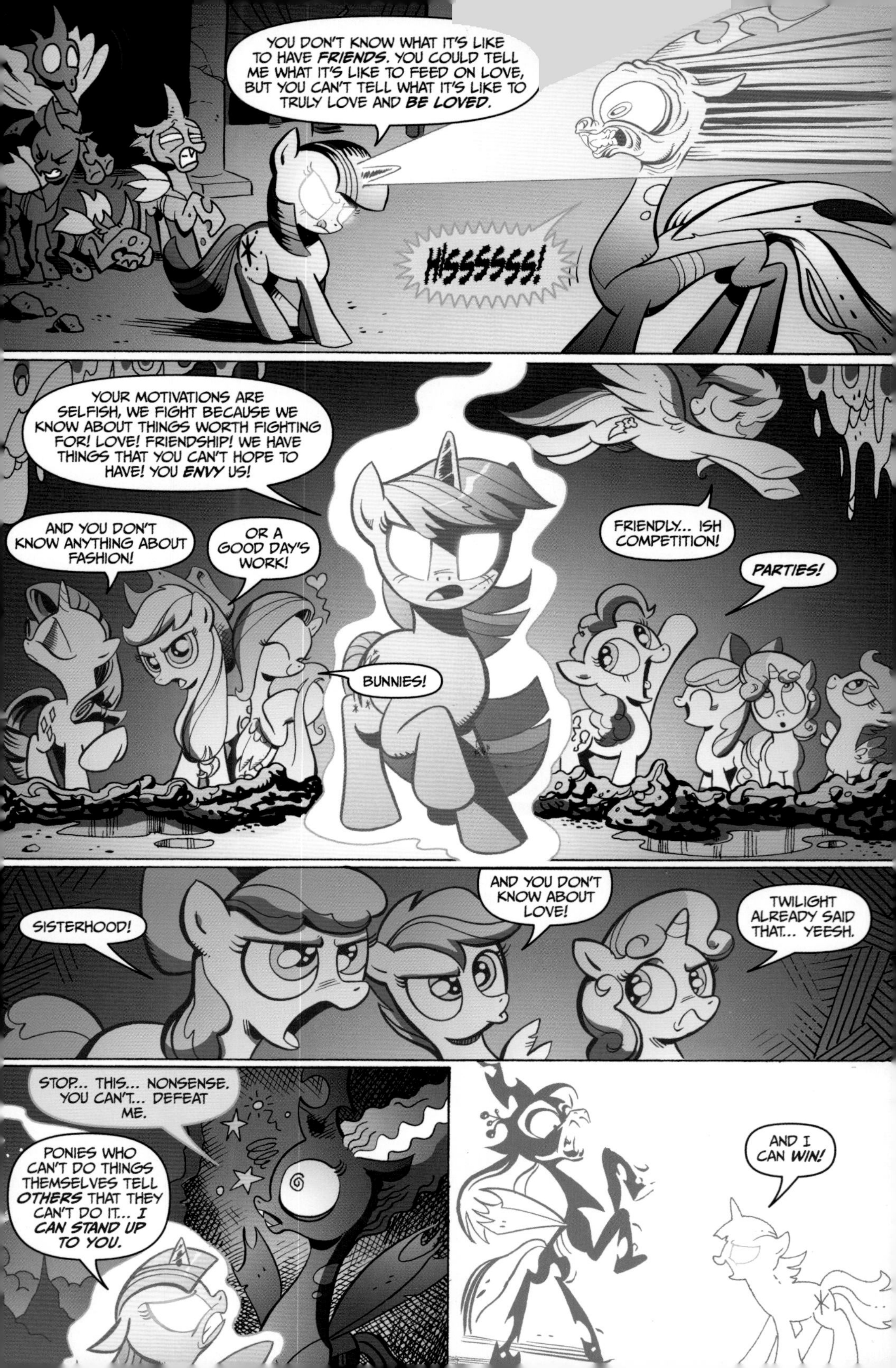
YOU DON'T KNOW WHAT IT'S LIKE TO HAVE *FRIENDS*. YOU COULD TELL ME WHAT IT'S LIKE TO FEED ON LOVE, BUT YOU CAN'T TELL WHAT IT'S LIKE TO TRULY LOVE AND *BE LOVED*.
HISSSSSS!
YOUR MOTIVATIONS ARE SELFISH, WE FIGHT BECAUSE WE KNOW ABOUT THINGS WORTH FIGHTING FOR! LOVE! FRIENDSHIP! WE HAVE THINGS THAT YOU CAN'T HOPE TO HAVE! YOU *ENVY* US!
AND YOU DON'T KNOW ANYTHING ABOUT FASHION!
OR A GOOD DAY'S WORK!
BUNNIES!
FRIENDLY... ISH COMPETITION!
PARTIES!
SISTERHOOD!
AND YOU DON'T KNOW ABOUT LOVE!
TWILIGHT ALREADY SAID THAT... YEESH.
STOP... THIS... NONSENSE. YOU CAN'T... DEFEAT ME.
PONIES WHO CAN'T DO THINGS THEMSELVES TELL *OTHERS* THAT THEY CAN'T DO IT... *I CAN STAND UP TO YOU.*
AND I CAN *WIN!*

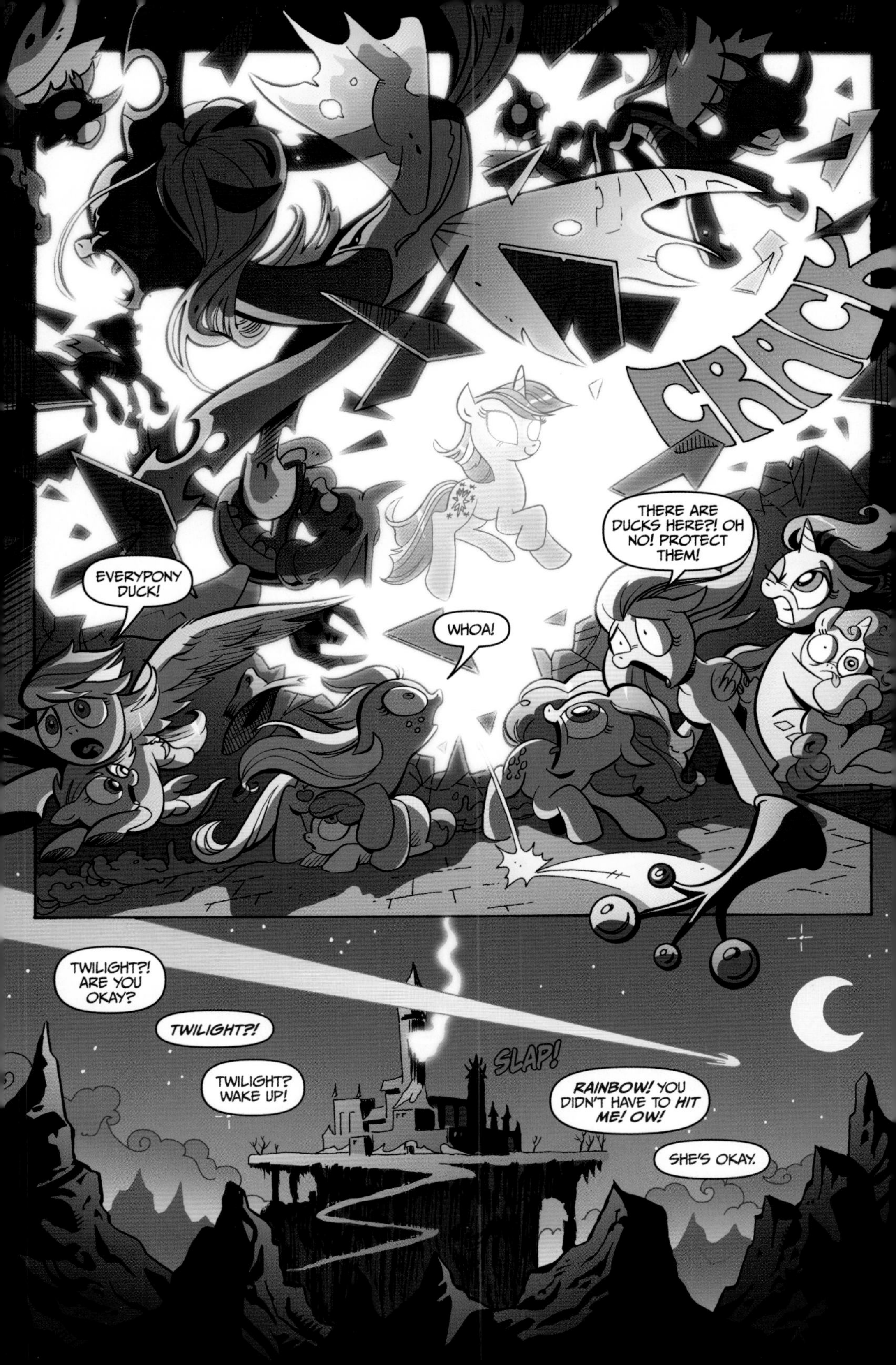

CRACK
EVERYPONY DUCK!
WHOA!
THERE ARE DUCKS HERE?! OH NO! PROTECT THEM!
TWILIGHT?! ARE YOU OKAY?
TWILIGHT?!
TWILIGHT? WAKE UP!
SLAP!
RAINBOW! YOU DIDN'T HAVE TO HIT ME! OW!
SHE'S OKAY.

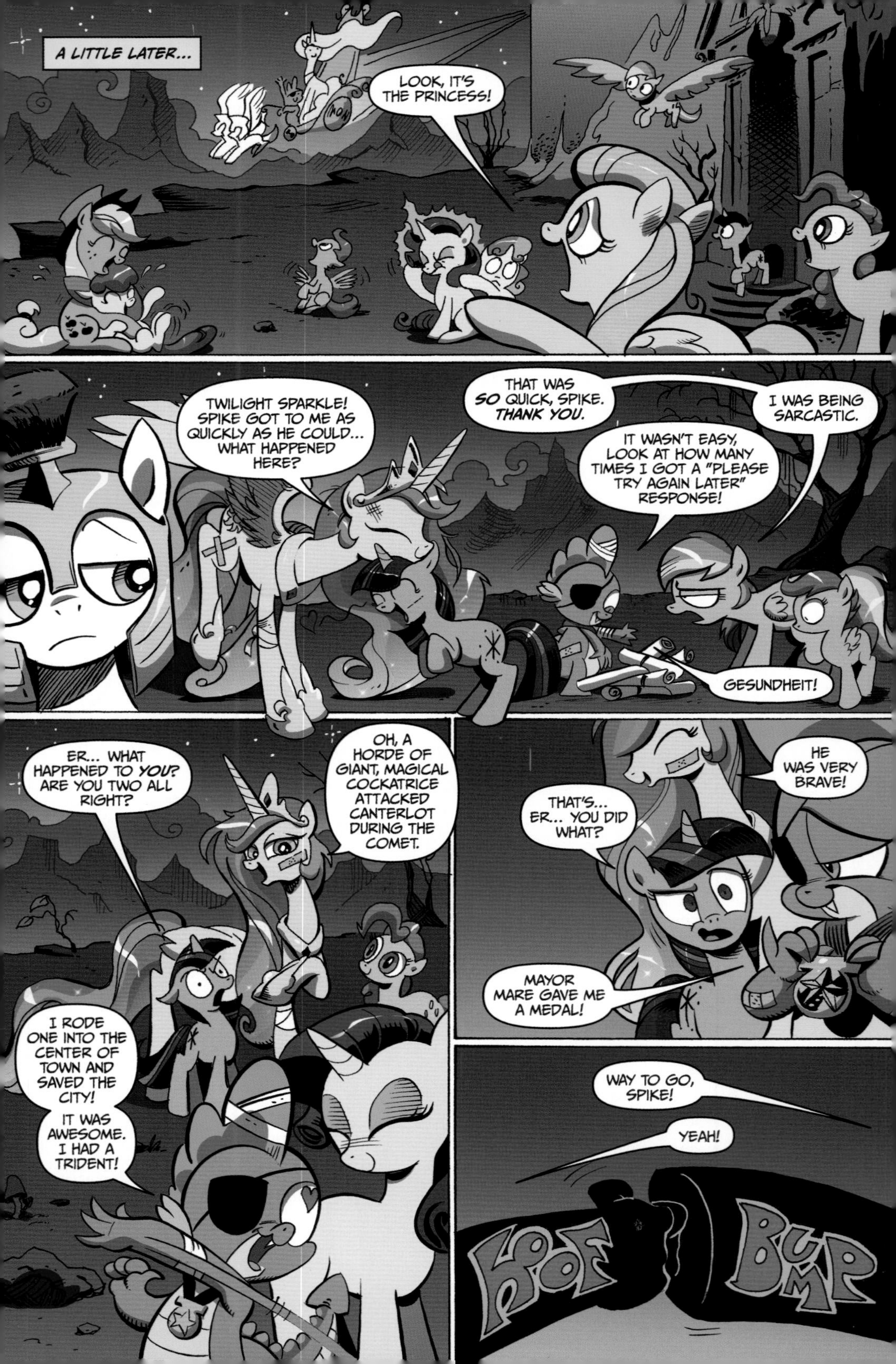

A LITTLE LATER...
LOOK, IT'S THE PRINCESS!
TWILIGHT SPARKLE! SPIKE GOT TO ME AS QUICKLY AS HE COULD... WHAT HAPPENED HERE?
THAT WAS SO QUICK, SPIKE. THANK YOU.
I WAS BEING SARCASTIC.
IT WASN'T EASY, LOOK AT HOW MANY TIMES I GOT A "PLEASE TRY AGAIN LATER" RESPONSE!
GESUNDHEIT!
ER... WHAT HAPPENED TO YOU? ARE YOU TWO ALL RIGHT?
OH, A HORDE OF GIANT, MAGICAL COCKATRICE ATTACKED CANTERLOT DURING THE COMET.
I RODE ONE INTO THE CENTER OF TOWN AND SAVED THE CITY!
IT WAS AWESOME. I HAD A TRIDENT!
HE WAS VERY BRAVE!
THAT'S... ER... YOU DID WHAT?
MAYOR MARE GAVE ME A MEDAL!
WAY TO GO, SPIKE!
YEAH!
HOOF BUMP

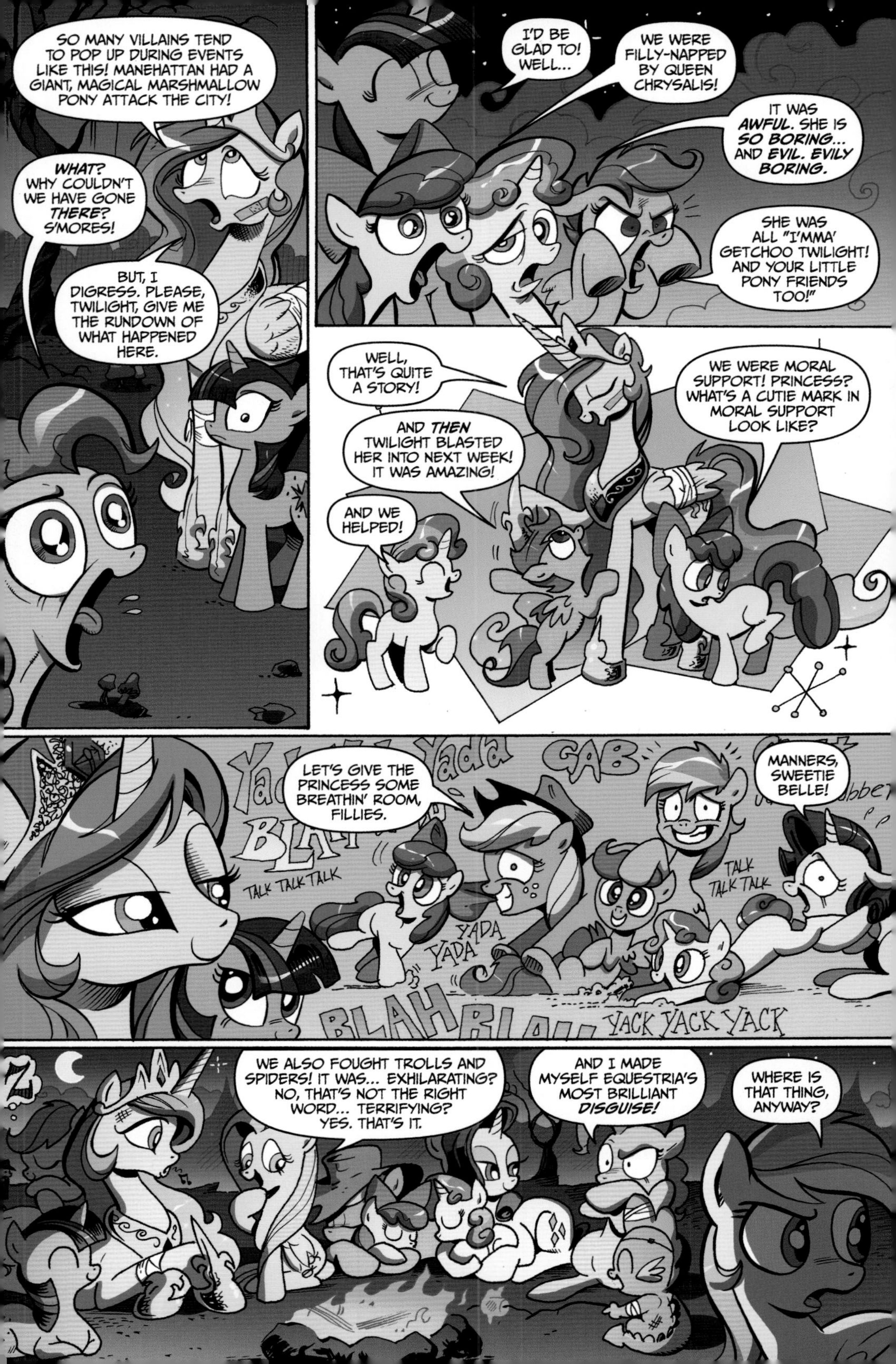
SO MANY VILLAINS TEND TO POP UP DURING EVENTS LIKE THIS! MANEHATTAN HAD A GIANT, MAGICAL MARSHMALLOW PONY ATTACK THE CITY!
WHAT? WHY COULDN'T WE HAVE GONE THERE? S'MORES!
BUT, I DIGRESS. PLEASE, TWILIGHT, GIVE ME THE RUNDOWN OF WHAT HAPPENED HERE.
I'D BE GLAD TO! WELL...
WE WERE FILLY-NAPPED BY QUEEN CHRYSALIS!
IT WAS AWFUL. SHE IS SO BORING... AND EVIL. EVILY BORING.
SHE WAS ALL "I'MMA' GETCHOO TWILIGHT! AND YOUR LITTLE PONY FRIENDS TOO!"
WELL, THAT'S QUITE A STORY!
AND THEN TWILIGHT BLASTED HER INTO NEXT WEEK! IT WAS AMAZING!
AND WE HELPED!
WE WERE MORAL SUPPORT! PRINCESS? WHAT'S A CUTIE MARK IN MORAL SUPPORT LOOK LIKE?
LET'S GIVE THE PRINCESS SOME BREATHIN' ROOM, FILLIES.
MANNERS, SWEETIE BELLE!
Yada
GAB
TALK TALK TALK
TALK TALK TALK
YADA YADA
YACK YACK YACK
WE ALSO FOUGHT TROLLS AND SPIDERS! IT WAS... EXHILARATING? NO, THAT'S NOT THE RIGHT WORD... TERRIFYING? YES. THAT'S IT.
AND I MADE MYSELF EQUESTRIA'S MOST BRILLIANT DISGUISE!
WHERE IS THAT THING, ANYWAY?

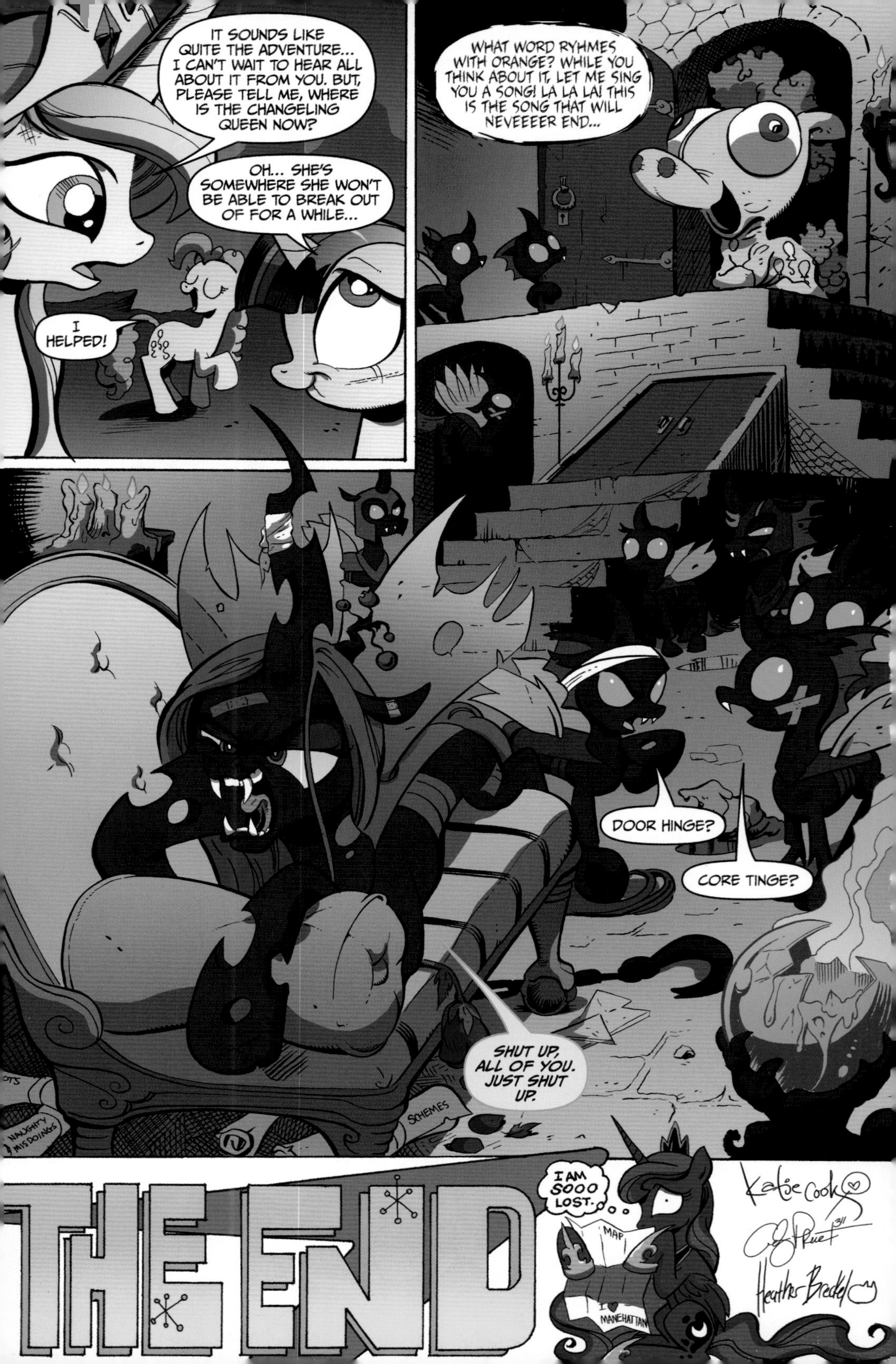
IT SOUNDS LIKE QUITE THE ADVENTURE... I CAN'T WAIT TO HEAR ALL ABOUT IT FROM YOU. BUT, PLEASE TELL ME, WHERE IS THE CHANGELING QUEEN NOW?
OH... SHE'S SOMEWHERE SHE WON'T BE ABLE TO BREAK OUT OF FOR A WHILE...
I HELPED!
WHAT WORD RYHMES WITH ORANGE? WHILE YOU THINK ABOUT IT, LET ME SING YOU A SONG! LA LA LA! THIS IS THE SONG THAT WILL NEVEEEER END...
DOOR HINGE?
CORE TINGE?
SHUT UP, ALL OF YOU. JUST SHUT UP.
NAUGHTY MISDOINGS
SCHEMES
THE END
I AM SOOO LOST.
MAP
MANEHATTAN
Katie Cook
Heather Breckel

my LITTLE PONY™
Friendship is Magic 2

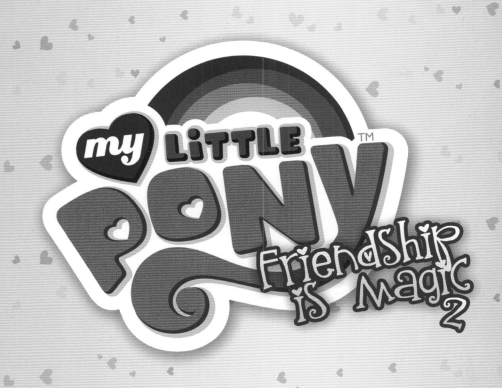

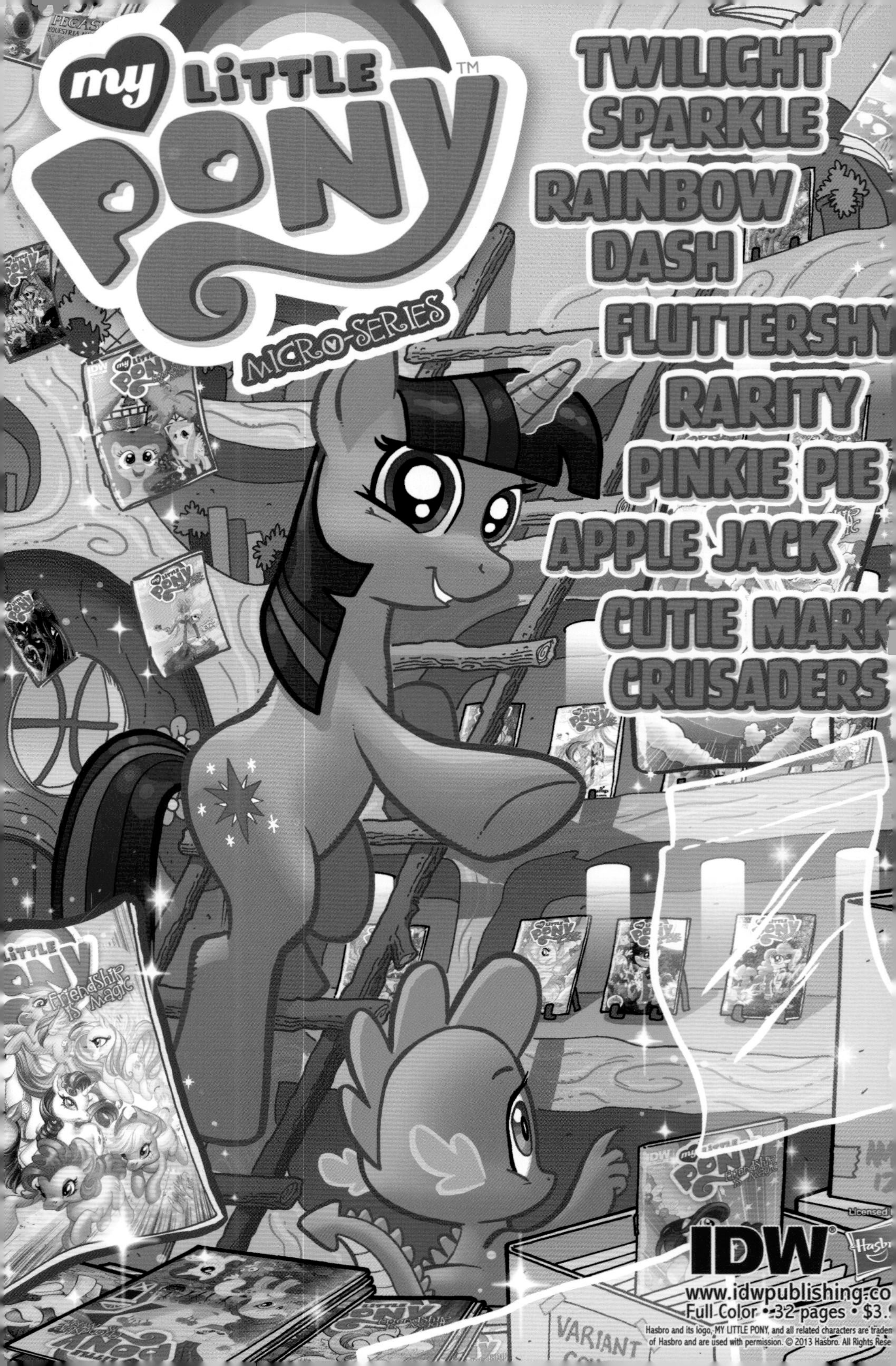

my LITTLE PONY™
MICRO-SERIES
TWILIGHT SPARKLE
RAINBOW DASH
FLUTTERSHY
RARITY
PINKIE PIE
APPLE JACK
CUTIE MARK CRUSADERS
Licensed
IDW®
www.idwpublishing.co
Full Color • 32 pages • $3.
Hasbro and its logo, MY LITTLE PONY, and all related characters are tradem
of Hasbro and are used with permission. © 2013 Hasbro. All Rights Rese
VARIANT